AMBUSH

Sam squatted behind a boulder, where he had a clear view of the ravine. He held perfectly still, relaxing, tensing only the muscles needed to hold him in place. It was a silent and invisible posture, a way to wait that the Apache had taught him years ago.

If you crouched down, or even just tried to remain immobile for any length of time with muscles tensed, it wouldn't be long before your body began to ache, cramp up painfully on you. But relaxed, focusing on his breathing and the world around him instead of himself, Sam felt he could stay in place forever.

Sinking into to it, alert to sounds, and temperature, and smells, and the touch of desert breeze, only his eyes moved as he scanned the hillsides for sign of more gunmen.

Rock Canyon Massacres

A Sam Colder Adult Western

Kurt Dysan

Kurt Dysan Westerns

"When the shooting stops, the last man standing isn't the winner... he's the survivor. A winner is the man who keeps the guns from blazing."

— *Sam Colder, bounty hunter.*

As reported by Claire Reed in the Chicago Tribune in her column: Gunmen of the West

Chapter 1

Mexican Bandits

Hearing the clatter of hoofbeats in the street below, Elmore Redding, mayor of Rock Canyon, reluctantly got up from his desk and went to the window of his office.

In the dusty street below him, in front of the general store, Sheriff Mark Douglas and his stocky, brutish deputy Tankheart Williams were pulling two Mexicans off their horses. The men, dirty, sweat-soaked, had their hands tied behind their backs.

Elmore thought they looked frightened.

He leaned out the window. "What's this, then, Sheriff?"

Douglas looked up and scowled. Redding knew the man disapproved of him, but increasingly, he didn't seem to care if Redding saw it. That was disrespectful, and it bothered him. He would have to mention the man's attitude to John Chancellor the next time he saw him. Chancellor would put Mark Douglas in his place quick enough.

"These fellas are the bandits been terrorizing the homesteaders, Mister Mayor. The ones that wiped out entire families."

"Bandits? These fellas hardly look like bandits. They look like scared rabbits more than bandits."

"They look scared as shit because we caught their dumb asses and they know they'll get hung," the sheriff said.

"I'm coming down," Elmore Redding said.

He grabbed his derby and headed out the door and down the outside stairs. It annoyed him to have to leave the relative cool of the office in the middle of the day, but he was the goddamn mayor and needed to see what was going on.

When he stepped out on the boardwalk, he noticed a third Mexican draped across his saddle. Tied to it. He was dead.

Douglas saw the mayor looking at the body and snorted.

"That one made the mistake of going for a gun," he said. "I shot the dumb fucker."

The uncomprehending looks on the faces of the two prisoners gave Elmore a strange, uncertain feeling. It was as if they didn't understand what was going on.

"Speak English?" he asked them.

They simply stared at him, eyes wide. Not for the first time, he wished he spoke some Span ish. But this was Arizona territory now, and the damn Mexicans needed to learn English.

"Why did you bring this body into my town?" Elmore asked the sheriff. "Probably ain't no reward on him. Probably no one even knows the man's name."

"Poncho," Williams said. "They are all named Poncho."

Redding ignored the deputy. "I don't need no dead Mexican stinking up the town."

"I wanted you to see him, is all. Wanted you to know we got all three of the murdering bastards."

"Why?"

"So you can wire the governor and tell him we got 'em, tell him we got this handled."

Douglas' interest in making the governor aware struck him as strange. Sure, the governor needed to know, but that had nothing to do with the sheriff, unless... hell, maybe the man thought the governor would give him a medal or something. Fat chance of that.

As Douglas pushed one man toward the jail, Williams grabbed the other by the arm and followed.

"Why would I wire the governor?" Redding asked.

"So he'll know we stopped the rampaging and killing out here. He can rest easy now," Douglas said, calling back over his shoulder.

"I'll lock these two up for tonight. We can hang them in the morning."

"What are you talking about? What's the rush?"

"Get 'er done and the town can save some money if we bury the three together in one big hole."

"You can't hang them without there being a trial," Redding said. "The governor wouldn't be pleased to hear about a lynching."

"Hey, I'm the law," Douglas said. "So it ain't a lynching."

"I know you've only been a lawman for a month, Douglas, but you aren't the law. You are the arresting officer. Only a judge can decide if men deserve to be hung." He brushed the dust off his pants leg. "Even Mexicans. Without a fair trial, it's a lynching. That's the law."

Douglas shook his head. "Damn shame."

"Maybe so."

"Well, if that's how it is, then tell them to send out the judge pronto. I'll have the undertaker deal with the dead one and stuff the other two in the jail to wait for him."

"I'll let Donna know that they'll be there for a time. She'll arrange for their meals."

"Tell Missus Redding that she only needs to fix beans and rice for these hombres," Douglas said. "They don't deserve no better."

Chapter 2

Changing Gears

Sam Colder toweled himself off and stepped out of the bath feeling refreshed.

"There are your clothes," Mary said.

Mary was a slender black woman, one of Thelma's girls. When he had shown up in Prescott, coming in off the trail, stinking of horse and sweat and endless campfires, Thelma had taken one look at him and sent him off.

"Get your ass over to your room at the boarding house," she said. "I'm sending Mary along to get you presentable," she said.

And she had. Mary had bathed him, shaved him, cut his hair, and otherwise refreshed him.

And now Mary was pointing at clothes she had laid out on the bed. The clothes he'd been wearing were piled up in the corner.

"Thelma wants you wearing those tonight," she said.

He looked at them and snorted. "Gambler's clothes," he said. "White shirt, fancy pants, and new boots... the whole deal."

"Gentleman's clothes," Mary said. "Thelma don't want you going into her fancy house dressed like some saddle tramp."

"But I am a saddle tramp," he said. "And I'm part owner of the damn place."

"So when you go there, you best look like an owner and not some bum who snuck in the place. No sense in scaring off the upmarket customers she worked so hard to attract. Besides, she wants you to meet someone."

Someone important, she meant. Important to her.

Thelma had surprised Sam with the deft way she managed their business. Going into business with her, funding it as a silent partner, had been a smart move. In no time, she'd made their idea of opening an upscale cat house a roaring success. It was all her vision.

Quickly, politicians and lobbyists, businessmen, and other big deal people learned they could trust her to see that people they wanted to be pleased were delighted. She'd combined it by opening The Bar T, a public bar, and made it an elegant meet-and-greet place where even the governor of the territory didn't mind being seen. And there was no scandal in eating in the attached restaurant, Thelma's, which become the finest in Prescott, the capital of the Arizona Territory.

Those two places were well known and completely legitimate. But, for exerting real influence over powerful men, that was just the start of Thelma's businesses.

When an elegant dinner wasn't enough, an elite group of members and their guests could slip off into a private half of the house. There, she offered a salon where the men could discreetly meet her hand-picked and specially trained girls. The girls provided attractive entertainments and a variety of intimate services.

In Prescott, and now in Tucson, when the rich and famous wanted to delight a customer, a powerful person, they took them to Thelma's.

"She needs you to blend in with her clientele," Mary said.

She was right.

On the bed, next to the white shirt, he saw a pistol. It was shiny, new, and small.

"What's this?"

Mary laughed. "A Colt New Line, dummy. Brand new."

"It's tiny," he said, hefting it, looking at it noting that the gun was loaded.

"A five-shooter. Looks like 38s."

"Thelma said she knows you'll feel naked going out without a holster on and she can't allow that, so carry this with you. In a pocket and out of sight."

He chuckled, imagining walking into the public bar with his guns on. The men in suits would be on edge, even if most of them carried a derringer.

"It's a lot better than the gentlemen's pop-guns they'll have," he said. "Most of them are 22 caliber. Hardly worth shooting. This one will put the hurt on a man."

"I'm sure glad that pleases you," Mary said, grinning. "I guess knowing you can hurt anyone in the place is a man's thing."

He shook his head. "Not so much, but knowing you can defend yourself is."

"I'll take your word for that, Sam," she said. "Me, I'm not pleased by all the killing that goes on."

"Being willing to kill ain't the same thing as being pleased by it," Sam said. "Not the same at all."

She grinned. "Well, I think I like you even better than I thought I did. And that is saying something."

She held up his coat. "Now it's time for you to have that business meeting with Judge March."

Chapter 3

Judge March

S am Colder sat in a comfortable leather chair at the table in the elegant bar, sipping an appropriately excellent whisky. A tall man in an expensive suit, muttonchops, and cool gray eyes that matched the color of his hair, moved toward him.

He felt good. The hot bath and hotter whore had washed away the trail dust and some of the frustrations of coming home empty-handed from his last venture. When his quarry had headed down deep into Mexico, taking a path across the searing Sonora desert, Sam had made the painful decision to let him go.

He had no interest in making a career out of running down one lone man.

Returning to Prescott let him find out how Thelma's venture was doing (excellently) and take a needed break.

Now, dressed in the fine clothing that Thelma had provided, feeling a bit awkward and out of place, he was waiting. He'd been waiting for this man... the man Thelma wanted him to talk with.

And drinking whisky. This very good whisky.

The man stopped at his table and looked down at him with the impatient, stern manner of someone used to wielding authority. Something in those eyes told Sam that the man knew he belonged in this place, in places like it wherever he went, and that Sam didn't. Not really. Men like Sam, when they'd been cleaned up a bit, could be allowed, tolerated. But they didn't belong.

He couldn't know that Sam was part owner and Sam didn't want him, or people like him to know that.

He glanced up and gave the man a smile.

"Can I help you, sir?"

"If you are Sam Colder... if you are him, I was told you could."

Sam motioned to an empty chair. "I am. And you must be Judge March?" The man nodded his gray head. "Thelma told me to expect you. Please join me."

"Thank you." The man settled into the chair, motioning to the waitress who clearly didn't need to ask for his order. Without missing a beat, she swept over to the bar and returned with a brandy.

"Here you go, your honor," she said, putting it in front of him. "From your private bottle."

Not just a judge, then—a man important enough that they kept his private stock right handy.

"Thank you, Evelyn," he said. "Bless you."

When she'd left, the man sniffed the liquid and took a sip. Rocking his head back, he inhaled through his mouth. Then he nodded. "I needed that."

"Rough day?"

"Rough week. Rough month, to be honest."

Sam waited, letting the man work up to saying outright what he wanted from him. There was no point in guessing what he wanted or rushing things. Men like this would get their hackles up if you let on you minded being kept waiting.

And he didn't, really. He found it different, novel having a judge looking for him.

"You know my name, but do you know who I am?" he asked.

Sam cocked his head. "You are with the high court, right?"

The man smiled. "Yes. That's right. Most people don't even know there are different kinds of judges." Then he laughed. "Of course, your line of work..."

"Bounty hunters get to know about some of that," he said.

"And a former lawman."

"In another life."

The judge sipped his brandy. Sam took a sip of his whisky and let it trickle down his throat. Fine stuff, indeed, even drinking with a judge.

"Another life," the judge said.

"I've lived a few," he said. That was an under-statement when he thought about it.

"Yet, you look more like... a gambler," he said.

Hearing his own thoughts thrown back at him made Sam laugh. "Do I now?"

"No disrespect meant. Your clothes are nice, but too elegant for a businessperson, much less a gunman."

"Gunman is a vague and useless term," Sam said. "It refers to most men out on the trail and they all got different aims, not to mention skills and attitudes."

The judge waved a hand. "I didn't mean any offense."

"And none taken. The term fits me, I was just making a point. And, as far as the clothes go, I'm not trying to pretend to be something I'm not, a respectable gentleman. A lady friend picked them out for me. It suited her fancy if I looked like I fit in, at least a little bit."

"And that lady friend would be Thelma?" he asked.

"The very same."

The judge nodded. "She said you were the right person to help me out. To help out the governor."

"The governor?"

"I've read a lot about you, Colder, and I still don't know much at all."

Sam laughed. "That damn fool book?"

He looked puzzled. "No. You are in a book?"

"A novel," he said.

The judge nodded. "Well, I was talking about newspaper articles."

Relief shot through Sam. He hadn't finished reading the book yet and didn't really know how Claire had portrayed him.

The judge held up his glass and winked at the waitress. Sam did the same.

"I had the editor of the Gazette compile articles he's written about you. There are quite a few. Some are even complimentary. Especially the ones in the Chicago Tribune."

More of Claire Reed's work. Sam grinned. "Good to know."

"The point, the reason Thelma asked you to have this chat with me, to hear me out, is that I, and the governor, need your help."

"I don't vote," Sam said.

"Well, that's an easy fix. But the issue ain't government, it's law enforcement."

"And you know, as we said, that was a past life."

"What I need is a special investigator," the judge said. "There have been some killings out around Rock Canyon."

"Never heard of the place," Sam said.

"Down near Nogales. A tiny town, only significant because it is surrounded by a few big ranches and a bunch of homesteaders."

"A dangerous mix," Sam said.

"Can be. Not always. But in this case, it might be. Entire families of homesteaders have been killed and buildings burned down. The remaining homesteaders are begging the governor to send troops to protect them."

"Tough thing to do, the way we scattered the homesteads out."

"Plus, it means taking troops from places we need them the next time the Indians rise up again... as they do."

"That being Chiricahua Apache territory makes it trickier," Sam said. "Sending in soldiers might upset them all by itself."

"And yet, the governor can't do nothing. He can't let someone slaughter those people."

"Hard call. But the fact that we are talking about this means you want me to get involved somehow. You didn't arrange this meeting so two gentlemen can just chew the fat about regional problems."

The judge laughed. "In short, get on with it. Well, it happens that the mayor of Rock Canyon, a fella named Elmore Redding, has hired himself a new sheriff. He claims they are sure the problem is Mexican bandits coming up across the border. He wired the governor, saying that this new sheriff is gonna take care of that problem."

"And, naturally, he is positive it's Mexicans and not Indians or maybe even the cattlemen who don't much like the homesteaders putting up fences and enclosing grazing land?"

The judge smiled wryly. "That's what he says."

"But you ain't so sure?"

"I've advised the governor that we need independent eyes on the situation. He agreed and asked me to find someone who doesn't have a stake in this squabble to poke his nose into it. He wants someone who can handle himself in a mess like this, with people like this, to look around let him know what is really going on."

Sam sighed. "And you are telling me this because you think I might be that fella? A little bird hinted you might persuade me to hightail it down there and sort this out?"

The judge sipped his drink and gave Sam a thin smile. "You come highly recommended."

"Thelma," he said.

"I checked you out and I think she's right. You've worked for both the Texas Rangers and Pinkerton's so you understand evidence and know how to conduct an investigation. You did well in those jobs. As well as a man can who just doesn't like dealing with the bu-reaucracy they involve."

"Working for the governor sounds pretty damn bureaucratic to me, Judge."

Showing the wisdom of his years of experience on the bench, the judge let that sit unanswered for a minute. Probably considering his answer. Noticing the way Sam fingered his empty glass, turning it, the judge waved at the waitress, who rushed over to refill it.

Sam gave her a smile.

"Sam, if you go down there, you would represent the governor and be able to use that as leverage, but you'll work for me. And I ain't asking you to fix all the problems in Rock Canyon. All I need you to do is find out what is really going on. The Territory is seeing some changes. Some political, some economic. We need law and order to prevail, at least some of the time, and I know you support that and always have, even as a bounty hunter."

It was true. The judge was picking at his weak spot, and he was sure he could blame Thelma for that. She'd prepared the judge for the meeting.

"Ask me any questions you like, and I'll do my level best to answer," the judge said.

"If this works out, if I can sort things for you, then you'll be leaving the bench, won't you?"

The judge laughed. "So the real question is what I get out of this?"

"Pretty much."

"It's true that with all that's happening, the governor is looking for people to work with him, people who prove to him they can make things happen. He wants people on his team who can pick competent people to do difficult jobs. He's looking for men who think the way he does to represent us in Washington. I can't say that isn't a motivation."

"Sitting here in this nice place, sipping the finest whisky this side of the Pecos River, chewing over the way things are, this job looks that simple. A man goes down around the border, talks to a few people, works out who is telling the truth and who ain't, and sends a telegram back with what is sort of a verdict."

The word choice made the judge wince. "Sort of a verdict."

"The reality of things in wilder parts of the territory is that a number of people might object to a man doing that very thing—poking his nose into what they will consider their business."

"Which is why I need someone who knows how to deal with that."

"Someone good with a gun."

"More than that," the judge said. "I'd prefer it to be someone who doesn't need to kill anyone who don't agree with him."

"Even if a man has the best of intentions on that score..." Sam scowled. "I need to know that you and the governor accept that an 'investigation' into what's going on might not please everyone. It could lead to a little bloodshed."

"I do know that."

"And the governor?"

"He accepts that might be the cost. If it's the ranchers, they will see you as a threat to what they see as their way of life. If it's Indians or Mexicans, well, kind of the same, I guess. But we have to know."

The judge was no idiot. "And of course, stirring these troubles up could make trouble for the governor. Say, at election time."

"It could. So could letting them fester."

Sam's gaze caught the judge's eyes. "So, that means we got to consider that whoever is behind the massacres might not be a rancher, Indian, or a Mexican."

Surprise flickered in his eyes. "I suppose so. Just someone who might benefit from a shitstorm down there and don't mind it costing innocent lives."

Sam sat back, letting all the thoughts, guesses, concerns that were floating around settle down.

"So my role, what we'd tell folks, is that I was sent down there as an investigator to look into who caused the massacres?"

"A special, independent investigator appointed by the governor. Not subject to whatever the sheriff has already decided."

"And I report only to you?"

He nodded. "As the governor's representative, who is looking into these troubles for him."

"This isn't the only hot spot, then?"

"I wish it was. We live in volatile times."

Sam smiled. "For those of us who have lived our lives in the territories, life has always been what you call volatile, judge. But when you push civilization, propriety onto frontier people, you got to expect some pushing back. And that's what you got, whether it's ranchers, Mexicans, or Apaches, doing the pushing."

As Sam's words sank in, a tinge of sadness that touched the man's face told Sam all he needed to know.

"Damn your hide, Judge. In your heart you miss the wild and woolly days, too," Sam laughed.

"You see through me, Mr. Colder. Them times wasn't always fair or just, but they was simpler and often easier to deal with. Especially when I was younger and tougher."

Sam was sure Judge March was still a tough old bird. Especially mentally.

"Back a few years, life out here was a struggle, more about life and death… survival, and a lot less about them other things like justice."

"Nowadays, we all got to agree on right and wrong," the judge said. "We got so many people who can't protect themselves from predators. We got a lot of people coming in expecting, demanding all the fine things civilization offers. And when that happens, well, it all changes."

Seeing how the man's eyes agreed with his words, Sam made two decisions. One was that he liked the judge. They wouldn't be good riding together, but Judge March was, in his mind, the kind of man the Territory needed to weather the unsettling, uncomfortable changes that would come with the transition from frontier to civilization. The kind of man who should be advising the governor.

And the other decision?

"I can leave tomorrow," he said. "It's a long way, but I'll ride down to Tucson, take a breather and rest my mount, then make the rest of the ride."

"Why the break?"

Sam smiled. "Seems my little investigation ain't just into who massacred those people."

"No?"

"From what you've said, much as I hate it, I got to consider the political aspects of things. I'm going to be interested to see what sort of stir my presence makes in Tucson because if I was a political person with connections in Prescott and I didn't want an investigator poking into local affairs, I'd make damn sure he didn't ever reach Rock Canyon. I aim to give them a variety of chances to do that, as it will tell me a little about who I'm dealing with."

"You're much more than a bounty hunter, Colder."

Sam grinned. "Don't give me too much credit, especially not until we sort this. But you might consider giving a lot of credit to someone else."

"Who?"

"Think about who it was who picked two warriors, two completely different kinds of men, and decided they could work well together for a greater good."

The judge looked puzzled for a time, then smiled. "Thelma."

"Keep an eye on her. She is part of the next generation of politicians, Judge. Look close and you'll see the future of this territory."

"Then we should drink to Thelma." He winked. "And I will keep that reference in mind."

"It never hurts to drink to a good person," Sam said.

At least, he couldn't think of a time he'd regretted doing that.

Chapter 4

Thelma and Claire

When Sam came back to his room in the boarding house, he found Thelma there, sitting in a chair, drinking a whisky and reading a book.

"Glad to see you made yourself at home," he said.

"If would have been easier if you had taken up my offer to have a room in my house," she said.

"Well, while I love how you've fixed the place up and how popular you've made it, I need a little space away from it where I can wear my trail gear and generally be rude," he said. "All that upper-class stuff, being polite and all, plumb wears me out."

"I was talking about my house, not living at the business," she said.

Then he remembered that Thelma had bought a smaller house down the street. She had wanted a place where she could live a public, genteel life.

"You and I are too close to being a married couple as it is," he said. He tugged at his shirt. "I got to put up with you picking out my clothes and telling me who to drink with."

He scowled at her, but she laughed and waved the book.

"You sound a lot like the man this book is about," she said.

"Do I now? I ain't had time to read it yet."

"It's about a bounty hunter. A damn good one, too."

"Well, ain't that something?"

"It's called Colder's List, because the guy makes lists of outlaws he wants to bring down."

"Does he now? He is some kind of a self-appointed lawman?"

"Just a bounty hunter, but he's also quite the lady killer." She held up the book. "Says here that just in this adventure, he manages to bed the mayor's wife and a couple of other women as well. And that's just in that town." She licked her lips. "Sounds like quite the stud. I get the distinct impression that the lady who wrote the book might know a thing or two about that part."

"Does it say that? Heck, them fiction writers stretch the truth something fierce."

"So it isn't true? This Colder fella didn't fuck the banker's wife."

"Well, he didn't bed her. That's just careless of her to write that when she knows damn well that what happened was that he fucked her on a desk in the bank."

"Who is she, Sam?"

"Who? The banker's wife?"

Thelma sipped her whisky.

"You know damn well I mean this Claire Reed. Who is this woman?"

"You ain't jealous, are you?"

"Would I fix you up with my best whores if I was the jealous type?"

"No. But somehow this is different."

She nodded. "I'm curious because she knows the man in that skin. She had to, in order to write this book about a fictitious bounty hunter named Sam Colder."

"You think she captured me?"

"I do. And then there is this."

She held up the book, opened it to the flyleaf, and read.

"It says, 'To Sam, for his help, his support, and friendship.' And the dedication, she mentions her late husband as well as her appreciation of hearing the inside story direct from Sam Colder."

"I did read that part."

"So you told her the tale so she could write it?"

"In truth, she did a hell of a lot more than hear the inside story."

"What else did she do?"

"For one thing, she shot a man dead. A man who was trying to kill me."

Thelma dropped the book. "Who is this woman, Sam?"

"I was on the track of an outlaw and, I guess, the book tells you why I couldn't just grab his ass. She and her husband were there. He was researching gunfighter stories for newspapers. They stayed at the same guesthouse as me."

"But she wrote this book... not him."

"She was already writing books, too, and they got published under his name. When the outlaws killed him, well, she had an exclusive story to sell. Seems like she made herself a deal."

"I knew it!" Thelma said. "And this is a big thing, Sam."

"Just another dime novel."

"Yes, but one she got published under her own name. That's a big thing for any woman."

"Is it?" He scratched his chin. "Well, Claire Reed is one hell of a woman."

"I want to meet her."

Sam laughed. "I'll write you a letter of introduction and you can go to Chicago and find her."

She shook her head. "I read that she's on a book tour."

"A book tour?"

"Traveling around the country promoting her book. It's quite a sensation."

"Is it now?"

"Did you know that up in Wyoming, women have the vote?"

"No shit? Well, why not?"

"Because a lot of men are afraid of women."

"Their loss."

"I'd like Claire to come to Prescott. As my guest. A group of women here get together to try to get the vote for us in Arizona territory. It would be inspiring to have a woman like that speak to us." She grinned. "She'd sell a powerful lot of books about a certain bounty hunter, too."

Sam wasn't so sure having books about him all over the place appealed to him, but he saw Thelma's point. He went over to the dresser and poured a whisky from the bottle.

"Write to her," Thelma said. "Ask her to come here. I'll give her a place to stay." She grinned. "In my house."

Sam sighed. Seeing Claire again would be good and whether he was tickled to having people reading about him or not, it was done. She couldn't take it back if she wanted to, and he was sure she didn't want to.

"She's an independent cuss," he said. "But I need to thank her for sending the book. I can tell her how the lady that owns the best whorehouses in the territory wants her to come talk to women about getting equal rights."

"Such elegance, Sam," she said.

"Of course, with the life she is carving out for herself, she might not be willing to settle for a low bar, like being equal to men. When she goes to battle, she aims to win."

"Sam, you just write the damn letter and let me deal with the politics. I'll even pay for the stamp."

"Damn right, you will."

Sam sipped the whisky and looked at Thelma. He liked her and respected her, and in that instant, he started to understand her.

"Your plan, right?"

"What do you mean?"

"This upper–class cat house, with its public face, all separate, the idea of wining, dining, and entertaining the rich and powerful... I thought it was a business opportunity."

"It is. And it's paying off."

"And, more importantly for Thelma, it puts her in a position to whisper in the ears of powerful men. It lets you jump into the world of politics yourself. And it don't matter one damn bit if you can't vote, for that part. But it also means you can start pressuring men to give women the vote."

"And why not?" she asked.

"No reason not to," he said. "I just didn't see it before, is all. I thought it was pure business."

"Suffrage is the issue. For women, for blacks and Mexicans, men and women," she said. "And that's just the beginning."

Sam shook his head. "That's sure ambitious."

She tipped her head. "Do you disapprove?"

He smiled. "Hell no. I'd probably be in favor of only women voting if you could manage that. I don't think men have the right sense for politics."

"That's not what we want," she said firmly.

"No, I guess not. But it tickles me that you have those ambitions."

"Then you'll support my efforts."

"I don't know shit about that stuff," Sam said. "But I won't get in your way, and I won't put up with anyone else trying to stop you."

"And you'll write to Claire Reed for me?"

"I'll write to Claire Reed for me," he said. "But I'll mention the kind offer of a place to stay and help selling books, even if I think she makes her heroes too good and the villains too bad."

"It sells books," Thelma said. "It's what readers want."

"And it would be nice if it was that way. The thing is, if I compare myself to the fella in that book, I get the feeling I come up short."

Thelma laughed. "A man's vanity is so fragile."

"Maybe so, but it's mine."

"You going to head down to Rock Canyon for the governor and Judge March?"

He refilled his glass and held up the bottle questioningly. She shook her head.

"Will it get you some political credit if I do?"

She stared. "Might. If you don't fuck it up, that is."

"It's a long ride down to the border," he said. "Not an easy one."

Thelma touched her hair, brushing it back, tossing her head, and looking at him differently now.

"You know, we are just setting up some girls at the house you bought in Tucson," she said.

Sam put down his glass and walked around behind Thelma's chair. He put his hands on her shoulders and bent his face to her ear.

"That so? Quick work."

"We hired a little redhead that I'm told fucks like a mink. You might need to stop off there for a day or so and find out if that's true or not."

"Finding things like that firsthand is always the best," he said. "But I'll be leaving tomorrow."

He dropped the Colt on the table beside her. "Hold this for me. Along with the fancy clothes. I'll need them when I get back."

She caught her breath. "You want me to send over one of the girls for the night?"

He put a hand down, slipping it inside her dress and cupping a breast. "How about you staying the night?"

"You like variety, as I recall."

"At times, but I like the idea of mixing a little business and pleasure too," he said. "Before I stick my neck out for your political ventures, I'd kind of like to stick my hard cock inside you a few times."

"You are a tough negotiator, Sam Colder," she said softly.

"And you are a sweet talker," he said. "But I happen to know you are also a sweet cocksucker and that makes it all right."

She stood to undress for him, silhouetted by the moonlight coming in the window, and then helped him shed those fancy clothes she had picked out for him.

When he was naked, he stretched out on the bed and watched as she took his throbbing tool in a delicate hand and stroked it, and licked it. And when he was sure he was going to go insane, she took it in her mouth to suck it.

Being in business with Thelma was definitely a fine thing.

Chapter 5
Ambush

Crossing the territory from Tucson to No-gales, often you could stare out across the harsh landscape and see little more than alkali sand, some cactus and scrub, and above him, a solid blue sky that sported one or two soft clouds.

And now, Sam Colder watched winds high up, winds he couldn't feel on his dry, sun-baked face, tearing those scarce puffy clouds into streamers.

Nothing else moved out there as far as he could see, which, on this flat space, was a long distance.

The land sat quietly, as if it waited patiently, expecting something to happen.

Sam was happy with nothing happening. Life was more peaceful when it left him alone with his thoughts. But even mired deep in wondering, thinking about things as far apart as Rocky getting older and wondering what he'd do when his horse was too old for this life, all the way to Thelma and the political bent she was showing. Still, he was alert, responsive to any sound or movement that might mean trouble, or simply something that needed his attention.

As he approached the foothills of the mountains that separated Fort Huachuca from Nogales, things came to life somewhat. A pair of red-tailed hawks circled lazily, riding a thermal up to an altitude they deemed perfect for hunting. They seemed to be concentrating their attention on a defile that led down the side of this mountain and then opened into an arroyo cut into the desert floor. It told a story of flash floods that came when the snow in the mountains melted.

This time of year, it was the ideal spot for a rabbit snare and the hawks seemed to agree.

Sure enough, one of the hawks let out a cry. Sam could imagine it shrieking, "Mine!"

Then it folded its wings and dove, swooping down, flushing what had to be a rabbit. But the rabbit headed back up the defile. Unwilling to fly into such a narrow passage, the bird climbed again, but its partner, likely seeing a wider opening further along the ravine, made its own dive, plummeting down.

Suddenly, it put out its wings, slowing its ascent, and then it, too climbed higher and the two banked, abandoning their hunt, and heading toward another part of the foothills.

A prickly sensation made his neck tingle. Taking a low breath, Sam dismounted and headed toward a small stand of withered trees that sat off in a slightly different direction. It was to one side of the trail that led through the mountains, the trail most men would take if they were traveling down from Tucson.

It took an hour to lead Rocky over to the grove, moving slowly and making a wide arc. As he'd hoped, the trees gave some protection from the sun, and the hint that there might be water there was true. Not much, but water. Enough to please Rocky.

Sam hobbled Rocky in the shade and then sat down and took off his boots. Even the hot, midday air was cool on his feet. He undid his bedroll and took a pair of moccasin boots he kept tucked in it, then sat on a rock and put them on. He liked his boots for riding well enough, but not for the scouting he needed to do.

As Rocky contentedly munched on some wild grass, he grabbed his Winchester carbine and scrambled up the hill. Going up and over, he could approach the ravine from partway down it, look down from the edge, rather than looking up at whatever, or whoever might be above him.

In the heat, it was a hard scramble. Not a difficult climb, just a lot of work, and it took a couple of hours of sweating and softly muttered curses to get into position.

But the climb was worth it. He emerged at the edge of the ravine looking straight down at a cowboy reclining against a rock with a carbine lying across his lap.

A bit lower down, two more were in what Sam considered shooting positions—concealed but close enough to the floor of the ravine that even an average shooter could pick off anyone riding through.

So the top one, the man not ten feet below him, was the lookout.

Sam squatted behind a boulder, where he had a clear view of the ravine. He held perfectly still, relaxing, tensing only the muscles needed to hold him in place. It was a silent and invisible posture, a way to wait that the Apache had taught him years ago.

If you crouched down, or even just tried to remain immobile for any length of time with muscles tensed, it wouldn't be long before your body began to ache, cramp up painfully on you. But relaxed, focusing on his breathing and the world around him instead of himself, Sam felt he could stay in place forever. Sinking into to it, alert to sounds, and temperature, and smells, and the touch of desert breeze, only his eyes moved as he scanned the hillsides for sign of more gunmen.

It seemed odd to be running across this ambush in the middle of nowhere. If the hawks hadn't alerted him to it, he might have ridden straight into it. But they had, and now he was in position.

Odds were he could easily kill two of the men before they even knew he was there. But this wasn't a time to shoot. It was a time to think about the men, the ambush.

No stage line or pony express ran through here, and he didn't know of any regular supply wagon that would pass this way either.

That meant these fellas weren't highwaymen, then, and that eliminated most of the reasonable possibilities. Fact was, it eliminated all that he could think of except for one.

Strange as it might seem, these boys had taken up these rather uncomfortable positions under the hot sun to wait for him.

It was flattering, but begged the question: who the hell were they?

Sitting this high on the slopes, their horses far away, the spots they'd chosen were ideal to shoot from. That meant they were waiting there to kill. This wasn't an attempt at capture.

If he could catch a glimpse of their faces, he might identify one or more. Maybe they were outlaws, friends of someone he'd shot or arrested.

That struck him as downright curious. Outlaws weren't known for this kind of revenge attack. It took too much effort and trouble. Sure, he had enemies. There were any number of men who would try to gun him down in a heartbeat if their paths crossed. But an ambush?

There wasn't money in killing him, as far as he knew, and this ambush was planned.

More interestingly, they knew where to wait. Knowing where he was traveling meant they had to have ears up in Prescott. Someone spotting him in Tucson wouldn't do it. When he left, he could be going anywhere at all, even El Paso.

No, somehow these boys knew that when he left Tucson, he would head this way, down around the Nogales area, and they'd arranged this little surprise.

Now he intended to make a chance to thank them and ask how they got their information. And from whom.

Meantime, he watched and waited.

Soon enough, it was clear these were cowboys. Gunmen, maybe, and probably outlaws, but not hunters. Sitting and waiting got them fidgety. They smoked cigarettes, which gave away their positions. They called out to each other. One fell asleep.

Boredom is a tough enemy to defeat.

After a time, the lookout called out and pointed to a cloud of dust.

"Wagon," he said.

The man was right. Even at this distance, Sam could tell it was a boxy wagon. Not a

Conestoga or buckboard. As it approached, he recognized it as one of the kind that carries medicine shows from town to town. The small towns loved them, not so much for the medicine, but for the show the people put on. The huckster pitches, the magic tricks which the adults would pretend amused the kids but loved themselves, and sometimes, in the evening, exotic dancers or puppet shows.

Having one arrive in town was an excuse to turn an ordinary day into a holiday.

Having one arrive here was a complication, but not necessarily a problem for Sam.

The two shooters saw the wagon and held a short discussion about it. Then one clambered up the hillside to the lookout.

"No sign of that fucking bounty hunter," he said.

"I sure ain't seen nothing," the lookout said. "And it's gonna get dark fast."

"Me and Chuck was thinking that wagon down there might give us some entertainment. The one like it we saw in Payson had pretty girls that danced."

"You want to make them dance for us?"

The man chuckled. "I was thinking it might be nice to have a pretty girl dance on my dick."

"Beats sitting up here in this damn heat," the lookout said.

"So, we gonna go down and get the horses. You climb down toward the front and when they enter the ravine, you tag along behind them. Ain't no room for them to turn around, but the people might make a run for it when we come out in front of the wagon and stop them."

"Well, as ugly as you and Chuck are, they just might run at the sight of you," the man said, chuckling. "Can't have pussy getting away from us. So let's do it." Then he paused. "What about the job? We been frying our brains for days. The boss said he was coming."

The man with the plan waved a hand.

"He guessed today, but it don't look like he's going to be getting here before dark. There ain't a spec on the horizon. We can take our positions early tomorrow morning."

"And wait in the scorching sun a whole other day? How long we gonna do that?" the lookout asked. "How long do we fry our brains out here before we decide he ain't coming at all?"

"The boss said he's coming. He'll probably mosey along tomorrow."

The confirmation that they were waiting for a rider put a lid on any idea he might be mistaken. And they were working for someone.

Sam saw life as a simple matter, and if these boys were outlaws out to settle a grudge, that told him it had something to do with the job the judge had given him. And that was likely why they knew he was coming and about when.

Someone in Prescott had let the cat out of the bag.

Sam calmed himself, and when the lookout started down the hillside, he followed silently after him.

He was glad he was wearing his moccasins.

Things were getting interesting.

Chapter 6

A Medicine Show

The hot rocks running down the sides of the ravine formed something of a switchback that made the climb down relatively easy.

Better yet, at the bottom, the ridge provided shelter. From there, he and the lookout both had a clear view of the wagon entering the defile, just squeezing through the narrow ravine. The lookout had his eyes fixed on the wagon. From behind him, Sam watched them both.

Getting closer, he could read the sign on the side of the wagon.

"Doctor Johnson's Miracle Cures & Madam Victoria's Fortune Telling and Exotic Dancing," it said.

It wasn't one he knew.

When the wagon was well inside the ravine, the two riders came out of hiding, riding up in front of the wagon.

"Greetings," the man driving the wagon called out. He was an older man in a black coat and his voice sounded cheerful, as he was glad to see these boys.

Next to him sat a tall, dark woman dressed in a cloak. With long, straight black hair and dark eyes, she wasn't Sam's idea of a beauty, but she definitely intrigued him. Her looks were exotic. Maybe that was the word.

The rider named Chuck leaned forward in his saddle.

"Well, now, that sign on your wagon looks interesting," he said. "You folks put on a show?"

"Wherever we go," the man said. "I'm Doctor Vaughn Johnson. The lady and I are on our way to Nogales to put on a grand spectacular. You should come to the show there tomorrow. As my guest."

"Well, we were thinking you might want to put on one of them shows for us right here," the man said.

"As nice as that sounds, I'm afraid we have other commitments," he said. "This is a well-known show, and we have bookings in Nogales and then further on, in Bisbee. We do operate on a firm schedule."

"Well, that ain't gonna work out so well for you," Chuck said. "We got your attention now, and we aim to keep it for a spell, seeing as we are starved for entertainment." He smiled at the woman. "Especially of the female type."

"I assure you that isn't possible," the man said. "We are expected."

As the lookout came up behind the wagon, Sam saw that the people in the wagon couldn't see him approaching.

With the lookout focused on the scene at the front of the wagon, Sam came up behind him and struck him with the butt of his rifle. The man collapsed and Sam caught him, pulling him behind the wagon and stretching him out on the ground.

When he peeked around the wagon again, Chuck had pulled out his colt and was pointing it at the doctor.

"And I assure you that we don't give a damn about what you think can and can't happen. In fact, you ain't even essential to our idea of entertainment, Doc. You are sort of a problem. But not a big one. Not something that I can't solve by simply putting a bullet in your head."

"That's not necessary," the man said.

"Didn't say it was," the man said. "I was just thinking that it would make things simpler. We wouldn't have to tie you up and keep an eye on you when we could be spending that time with your lady friend. I got some exotic dancing in mind."

"You are insulting the lady," the man said.

Chuck sneered. "And what are you going to do about it?"

The man looked astonished. "Me? Nothing at all."

"Well then," Chuck said.

A shot rang out and Chuck seemed to develop a stunned look at the same moment a hole opened up in his face.

Sam saw the second rider go for his gun. Sam fired, taking him out of the saddle. Almost in the same instant, another shot rang out. The woman had turned, firing in Sam's direction. Turning, he saw the lookout had recovered and come up behind him, but the lady had put a bullet in his chest, and he toppled forward.

Hearing hoofbeats, Sam turned again. The man he'd shot was back on his horse and riding away. It wasn't his day for putting men down.

Sam raised his rifle.

"Let the poor fella go," the woman said.

Sam lowered his rifle. Her smile made her more attractive than he'd thought.

"You don't want me to shoot him?"

She gave him an amused smile. "If it was a deer or other game animal, I'd insist, but I don't mind a wounded wild dog crawling off to die in some hole."

"But we thank you for the kind assistance, stranger," the doctor said.

"And my thanks for the help with the man I'd dealt with. Smacking him in the head with my rifle butt should have put him down for a spell, but I shouldn't have assumed that. I got a mite careless."

"It don't take much for careless to equal dead out here," the woman said. "And out here, outlaws tend to have particularly hard heads."

"That one was a tough devil," Sam said, nodding at the wounded rider disappearing down the canyon. "He's carrying my slug in his chest."

"His shoulder," the woman said.

"As you say," Sam said, grinning. "That was some nice shooting, Ma'am."

"Victoria," she said, letting the cloak open so he could see her Colt revolver.

"I hear you say you are headed to Nogales to put on a show?"

"Indeed, we are," the man said. "Doctor Vaughn Johnson, at your service. And, of course, Victoria is mistress of the unknown and unknowable, not to mention dancing."

"That's a lot to not know and not be able to know," Sam said, laughing.

The doctor winked and looked up at the sky. "We had hoped to make town by nightfall. However, that doesn't seem possible after this unscheduled interruption. But that's fine. It's been a rather long day and I'm thinking of pitching camp for the night." He pointed to a wide spot in the canyon. "That looks like a suitable spot."

"I think you are right," Sam said. "And even if that fella has friends, he's wounded and got some riding to do before he can get help."

"And some explaining to do as well," Victoria said, her voice flowing like a spring-fed river. "He'll have to tell whoever he works for that a woman shot his leader and the other man, and then he ran off without knowing the fate of either of them. It might take a few drinks in a faraway cantina to work up the courage to say that."

Doc Johnson shook his gray head. "He'll just say he and his friends ran into Mexican bandits and they got their asses kicked."

"What makes you think they work for someone?" Sam asked. "Why not just a gang of three?"

Victoria laughed like water flowing. "What's out here to rob?" she asked. "No, they were out here for a specific reason, and doing someone's bidding. We were just an opportunity they couldn't resist."

"While I dislike their means, the draw is certainly understandable," Sam said.

"Why thank you, sir... I think."

"I left my horse outside the canyon. I'm going to take this dead man's horse and ride around to where I stashed him," Sam said.

"We caught us some squirrels earlier, and we've got beans and potatoes," the doctor said. "You'd be welcome to join us for dinner." His eyes danced. "I just might have a little liquor tucked away as well."

"That's the best offer I've had in days," he said.

By the time Sam fetched Rocky and returned, they'd set up a nice little camp. A fire was blazing under a stew pot and Victoria was cutting up wild onions.

The doctor had a bottle of mescal that they shared while the food cooked. Then, as they ate, Sam took the measure of them. Doc Johnson was clearly a con man. Not a swindler, just ready to play a game that would enrich him a little. And Victoria... she was lithe and elegant.

The perfect con man's distraction.

"You mentioned those outlaws claiming they ran into Mexican bandits... you seen much of them in your travels?" Sam asked over dinner.

"Mexican bandits?" Doc Johnson asked. He shook his head. "Not so much. They are just the bogeymen."

"Boogeymen?"

"The fairytale bad guys. The people you blame everything on them because they are not around to deny it."

"I don't know about them being a fairytale. Word is a band of them been killing homesteaders sort of at random. Not so much here, but up around Rock Canyon."

"We don't get up there much," he said. "Not enough people in Rock Canyon to make it worth the while. It's more of a depot than a town. We heard that regular folks only go there to buy goods. Local cowboys and farmers keep the saloon in business. Nogales is more to our liking."

As Vaughn opened the mescal bottle to re-fill their glasses, Victoria gave Sam a penetrating look.

A smart woman lived behind those eyes. Maybe not educated, but smart and clever.

"Well, I was hoping you might have seen or heard something that might shed a little light on them killings," Sam said.

"Afraid not. And we pay attention to rumors of such things," Vaughn said. "We prefer to give danger a wide berth." He laughed. "I don't much like narrow canyons for that reason."

Sam took off his gun belt and sat it on the ground. The night was growing cool, but the fire was warm. Sam undid his moccasins and pulled them off.

With a sly smile, Victoria grabbed up the plates and empty cook pot and headed for the wagon.

Watching her move away from them, Sam sighed. Even the way she walked was a dance of delight.

The good doctor rocked his head back, smiling when Sam took out a rolled cigarette and handed it to him. Vaughn took a burning stick from the fire and lit the cigarette, then held it for Sam.

As they took a long first draw and then exhaled, Vaughn shook his head. "No. I can't see them doing that," he said.

"What?"

"What you said before. About Mexican bandits raiding homesteads."

"Why not? I'd like to hear your thinking."

"Because they ain't all that brave. They sure don't like to risk coming across the border unless they got a juicy target. Them killing people would bring the US Cavalry on their asses. They wouldn't want that. And when I think about a homestead... there ain't nothing there. What would they get? A couple of horses and some livestock and a few chickens, maybe."

Victoria laughed as she came back to join them. "They ain't that stupid."

She had changed into a filmy dress that clung to her body.

As she sat down and poured herself a drink, Sam admired her profile in the flickering firelight. Out of the corner of his eye, he saw Vaughn watching him, smiling.

"What about you, Sam? Do you think Mexicans killed those people?" Victoria asked.

Sam shrugged. "I was told that the sheriff arrested a couple. I got no idea myself, but I was thinking the same as Doc here. Trying to see how that made sense."

With the fire starting to die, Vaughn stood and brushed imaginary dust off his pants.

"This old fella needs his rest," he said. "I bid you all good night."

"Night, V," Victoria said. "Sleep well."

And off he went.

"He is a good sort," Sam said.

"He is. Without him…"

Then she moved closer to Sam, then picked up a stick, and poked the fire with it.

"V taught me this kind of entertainment game. He gave me a future."

"You can't make a lot of money at it," he said. "And it's hard work, all that traveling."

"Oh, there's so much hard about it," she said. "Most folks couldn't stand it. Not long. But it saved my life."

"That sounds dramatic."

"I grew up in a sharecropping family in an area where farming was probably a bad idea from the git go. When I was a teen, my parents both died—from the work. I was looking at a future where I'd marry some stupid hick and we'd do the same… work the land, raise kids, and die young, hoping that the next life would be better. Then one day, when I was deciding I needed some other choice, V showed up. He set off on his godawful sales pitch, peddling his obnoxious medicines and it was magic. I watched him mesmerize people."

"That's a big word," Sam said.

"That's what they call it you know, when you can bewitch people with talk. Some fella in

Europe named Mesmer invented it and Doc Johnson made it his own. Anyway, that day, he asked me to pass the hat and I did. He gave me a dollar. I'd never seen a whole dollar before."

"And you were on the path."

"Well, he asked me about my family. When I told him my folks were dead, he asked me if I wanted to go with him. Said a pretty girl collects more money."

"And where did you learn the rest?"

She laughed. "The gypsy stuff?" She tossed her head. "V took me to New Orleans and paid a real gypsy to teach me enough to make it look good. She taught me the dancing, and even gave me a veil to use. The men love it when it flows over my body."

Sam was watching the rise and fall of her breasts. "No doubt. It's a lovely body. What I can see of it."

The firelight caught a wicked smile moving across her face. "Would you like me to dance for you, Sam Colder?" she asked, putting on a strange, exciting accent.

"Very much," he said.

Her hand went to her breast. "Well, out here, in the middle of nowhere, I can do a modified version of the dance I do in the show."

"Modified?"

Moving slowly, she stood and began moving to music that only she could hear. She twisted and her hands described arcs in the air. She danced with her eyes on him, her audience. And she moved close, letting her dress flow against his arm and face. Each time that happened, he smelled her heady, perfumed scent.

When she twirled, the dress flared out, and he saw her strong, lovely bare legs.

The top of the dress opened. He hadn't seen her do it, distracted by her legs, perhaps, but the top opened and exposed her moon-kissed breasts. They glowed... firm and lovely mounds.

Seeing that she had his attention, she released her hold on the dress and he watched, transfixed, as it slid down her body, leaving her naked.

He rolled out his bedroll, and she sat by him, smiling when his hand reached out to touch her leg, to stroke the smooth, exciting skin.

"You are a princess," he said.

"Am I? Then you must be my savage barbarian," she said.

Her hand went to his crotch and ran over his stiffening cock. He leaned back slightly as she undid his pants, then reached inside them to grip his now hard cock.

"How savage is your barbarian?"

"Extremely." Her tongue danced on her lips as she pulled his cock out, staring at it as she stroked it. "He looks to be a lusty animal, eager to ravage his princess."

They way his pulse pounded, that seemed right.

She turned away from him, getting on her hands and knees and presenting her bare ass to him. He touched her ass, then let his fingers trace the swollen lips of her pussy. When he slipped two fingers inside her, she gasped.

"If he intends to take her, all the helpless princess can do is offer herself to her conqueror, give herself to him."

"Oh, he intends to take her, all right," he said, dropping his pants and moving behind her.

His hand guided his swollen flesh into her, then he gripped her soft hips and pressed deep into her, feeling the silky caress of her cunt grasping his cock, and hearing the moan of delight that escaped her lips.

Rocking his hips, he filled her with his cock, pounding into her in a frenzy of desire.

And when she put her face down on the bedroll and put her delicate hand between her legs to cup his balls, he came, exploding inside her.

They lay together, touching, and it seemed like no time at all before she had him hard again.

This time she mounted him, his lovely rider working his cock inside her as he looked up at her face, firm breasts, and Orion shining down over her shoulder.

When she came, crying out along with the coyotes on the hillside, he rolled her over, pushed her legs back to her breasts, and fucked her hard, taking his conquest, being the barbarian she wanted him to be.

Chapter 7

Rock Canyon

After his pleasant night with Victoria, the two-day ride across empty scrub land to Rock Canyon seemed lonely.

For a time, Sam rocked in the saddle, fantasizing of another life. In this one, he owned himself a wagon and traveled with Victoria. Roaming the territory, seeing her dance every night, and then, after a good meal, fucking her by a campfire every evening.

Then he laughed at himself for indulging in yet another version of his desire to find a home.

That's all it was, of course, and the desire came up often, even now that he understood that living alone, his home a bedroll in the wilderness or in his saddle, was the only life he would ever have. Sam Colder was an outsider by nature. He never could make belonging to anyone or any place work for any length of time at all.

He guessed Victoria was the same. She wanted to be free to give herself to a man if and when she wanted to. A woman like her, fine as she was, couldn't belong to one man or one place, and she'd probably make a shitty wife. Almost as bad as he'd be at being a husband.

The life he followed, and the paths he chose, were hard and precarious, but following them was what made it worth living.

On the second day, the bright southwestern sun had just begun to fade as he rode into Rock Canyon. The town had enough buildings to be home to a few people, but, as he'd been warned, it wasn't a real community. Doc Johnson had pegged it—more of a depot than a town. A place where homesteaders and ranchers could buy supplies and a saloon where workers from the ranches and homesteads could blow off steam come payday.

It didn't have a church, a school, or any of the things most of the towns were getting these days.

A couple of men ran the stores and the stables. A sign told him that the telegraph office was in the general store, and that gave him a clue how anyone would have known he was coming.

The town did have a jail—a squat and ugly adobe building sitting right next to the clapboard saloon.

A man stood on the boardwalk in front of the saloon when Sam rode up. The man leaned back against the wall, legs crossed, smoking a cigarette, watching Sam approach with the shifty but clear-eyed stare of a gunman and the star of a sheriff pinned to his chest.

Recognition, mixed with surprise, crossed the man's face and his hand edged toward the butt of the Colt revolver in his holster and hovered there.

"Welcome to Rock Canyon, Sam Colder," he said. "I'm surprised to see you out this way."

Certainly surprised, but not at all pleased.

"Well, Mark Douglas," Sam said. "Well, I got to say I'm surprised, too. Never thought I'd see you wearing a badge."

"It's a strange world," he said.

Sam swung down off Rocky and tied his reins to the post holding up the ramada that fronted the saloon. Turning to look at the sheriff, he'd relaxed and moved his hand from his gun. He didn't pose an immediate threat. For now, the man was just watching him, biding his time.

If there was going to be trouble, it wouldn't be now.

"Last I heard of you was on a wanted poster. Now here you are... representing the law itself."

"Seems the fine folks of Rock Canyon were concerned about the mayhem that some outlaws, a handful of Mexican bandits, and the like, were causing. They decided it made a bit of sense to hire a man for sheriff who knew how to use a gun. A man who wasn't afraid to use it."

"Well, I reckon that would give the people in power a chance to sleep nights," Sam said. "That is, assuming they didn't have to worry that the man would point that gun at them."

Douglas laughed. "Now that would be a bitch of a thing, wouldn't it?"

"Guess it might."

Sam stepped up on the boardwalk and headed into the saloon.

"Been a dusty ride," he said. "Come on in and I'll buy you a drink."

"Right neighborly," Mark Douglas said, pushing off the wall and following Sam into the saloon.

It was a small, dusty place with a couple of rude tables and some homemade chairs. The bar was nothing but a thick slab of wood. A woman sitting behind it looked up when he came in, smiling at the sight of a stranger. He guessed her to be in her early thirties. She had a tired face that might have been pretty once but had grown worn and toughened by the hard life, by years of being bleached by the harsh sun and caressed by the dry desert wind.

"Well, hello," she said.

"Can you pour the sheriff and me a couple of whiskies?" he asked.

Her eyes went to Mark Douglas. Her smile faded briefly, then popped back. "I think I recall how that's done," she said.

Sam and Mark walked to the bar as she put the glasses on it and poured two healthy glasses.

"This here is Sam Colder," the sheriff said. "Seems he is working for the governor up in Prescott these days."

Sam appreciated that Douglas didn't pretend not to know why he was there.

"The governor's man?" she asked.

"Sam, this lady is Donna Redding, wife of the mayor. She also runs the saloon."

Sam nodded and smiled. "I take it you were expecting me? Word sure traveled fast."

"The major got a telegram saying that the governor's office was sending out an investigator," Douglas said. "We don't get many visitors here, so you showing up and not being him would be too much of a coincidence to suit me."

It would have been better, more helpful if the judge hadn't alerted them. But he probably figured that sending word ahead would open doors for him, let people know they should talk to him.

If he'd known that was the plan, he would have asked them not to. There was a good chance that the telegram was the very reason he'd come across the welcoming committee in the ravine, the one that ambushed Vaughn and Victoria.

Sam put coins on the bar. "Well, I promised the sheriff a drink," he said. "And you are welcome to one as well, Donna."

"That's kind of you," she said, turning and grabbing another glass. "Thanks, Sam."

A man in a suit came in the door. "Thought I heard a rider come in," he said. He walked over and put out a hand. "Elmore Redding, the mayor of Rock Canyon."

"And the owner of the saloon, the stores, and whatever else might be worth owning," Donna said.

While the words were the right ones, her tone of voice didn't suggest admiration for her husband's achievements. She sounded downright scornful to Sam's ears.

But Redding didn't seem to notice.

"Well, it's a small place, so that ain't much," Elmore Redding said.

Just as clearly, Sam could hear the pride in his voice.

"Ain't nothing, either," Sam said. He nodded to Donna. "I reckon the mayor needs a drink, too," he said.

The comment pleased the man. "Did the sheriff tell you the good news?"

"Good news? Not really."

"We barely got past 'hello,' Elmore," Douglas said.

The mayor rubbed his hands together. "Well, we are happy to tell you that your trip out here was a wasted effort."

"Was it now? And how is that good news?"

Elmore slapped Mark on the back, oblivious to the look of scorn the sheriff gave him.

"Sheriff Douglas has already apprehended the killers."

Sam took in the sheriff's self-satisfied grin. "Did he now?"

The mayor nodded vigorously. "Yes, he did. Caught hisself two Mexican bandits. Killed a third."

"And you got them in the hoosegow?"

The sheriff grinned. "Locked up tight."

"All we need is for the judge to let us hold a trial," Elmore Redding said. "But there's no real need for a judge to make the long, hard trip out here himself."

"There ain't? How do you hold a trial, then?" Sam asked.

"Well, he could appoint me as a judge for this case."

There was precedent for such things. Traveling the territory, getting a judge to every community that needed one was a challenge, and special circumstances often were accommodated.

"That's a fine offer," Sam said. "Now you'll need Judge March to decide, but he gave me the impression that he ain't too keen on passing along the responsibility for judging a hanging offense. And, since he asked me to look into things and send him my view on the evidence and the situation, I can mention that idea to him."

"Investigating any further is totally unnecessary, I assure you," the mayor said.

"Probably true. A lot of law stuff seems that way to me too. But it's what he asked me to do. He gave me strict instructions. Of course, if I poke around and decide you are right, in a few days I'll be able to wire him and tell him that you and Sheriff Douglas done a fine job of investigating and that he might as well do what you suggest."

"A few days?" Redding asked.

Sam shrugged and signaled for Donna to re-fill the glasses. "I came all this way and now, to give his honor what he asked for, I best talk to the prisoners myself."

"They don't speak much English," the sheriff said.

"I got me some passable Spanish," Sam said. "Good enough for this."

"That won't take long," the sheriff said. "You can do it in the morning. Come on in, chat with them, and you can head home."

"Well, I promised to be thorough. So I'll need directions to the site of the last massacre and to a couple of the ranches in the area."

"Ranches?"

"Yeah. The judge said I need to talk to some fella named Chancellor, and another named Evert, in particular. And I need to talk to a homesteader named Holloway."

"What for?" Redding asked. "You won't see much at the homestead place. They burned it to the ground. And why bother the ranchers? They ain't had a problem at all."

"And Holloway?"

Elmore Redding swallowed his whisky. "Sonofabitch is a troublemaker. Goddamn sure he knows what's going on and that there is some kind of conspiracy against the home-steaders."

Sam didn't answer right away. For the plea-sure of stalling the mayor, enjoying the man's frustration, he sipped his drink, letting the warm liquid trickle down his throat. Then, giving the man a smile, he looked him in the eye.

"Well, here is the truth of it, mayor. I got to do what strikes me as right. I got to do my own little investigation even if it's a waste of time. That means finding out if the ranch hands have seen bandits around, it means looking at the massacre site. That means listening to Mr. Holloway's take on things, too. Mostly, it means getting my own information and making up my own mind about what happened."

"What a waste," Redding said. "We could get on with this."

"If it's a waste of time, it don't hurt a damn thing. The governor will pay for the cost of feeding the prisoners while I do my work, and I'm being paid for my time. I was asked to come to my own conclusions about what happened. That ain't because of anything, except that neither of you is a trained lawman."

Sheriff Douglas gave him a sour stare. "And you are just a fucking bounty hunter, Colder. Why don't I wire the judge and tell him that the man he sent out to investigate ain't nothing more than a hired gun."

"Sure, why not?" Sam asked. "But as it happens, that is exactly what I told Judge March when he first asked me to take this job on. He thought my years with the Texas Rangers and Pinkerton's might be of some use, though." He smiled. "I reckon it's like the mayor here figuring out that your skills would suit being sheriff, even if you did mostly practice them breaking the law. He let bygones be bygones. So did the judge."

The scowl on Douglas' face deepened.

"Fine, you are welcome to talk to every man, woman, and child within a hundred miles, if you like," he said. "Ride all across the countryside and then come back and tell me we can hang the guilty men I got in the jail."

Sam sipped his fresh drink, then smiled. "Thank you kindly, sheriff. I'll do exactly that."

Then he turned his smile on Donna. "This saloon got rooms for rent?"

"We got a couple of simple ones right out back," she said.

"I'll take one for the night," he said.

"We got a stew on the fire," she said. "Dinner is extra."

"Sounds nice," Sam told her. "I'll need somewhere with shelter and food for my horse."

"A dollar a night," Elmore Redding said, switching easily into his town merchant role. "I'll have that Mexican boy come get him."

"That will be fine," Sam said. "Tell the boy his name is Rocky, and he likes to hear his name."

The mayor looked nervous. Edgy.

Sam turned back to Douglas.

"By the way, Sheriff, I'm curious about how you found the bandits."

Douglas puffed up. "Me and my deputy went out to the last massacre site and found some horse tracks leading up into the hills. We found the bastards camped up there, sitting around a fire and drinking some hooch they'd taken from the homestead, I'm thinking. We walked right into their camp and surprised them."

"And they went for guns when you came in?"

"One did. Hell, these men are bandits... desperadoes. I stepped into the light of the campfire to talk to them, and one tried for his gun."

The man's eyes narrowed. "Didn't work out well for him."

"I wouldn't think so, you being useful with a gun and all."

Douglas watched Sam's face, measuring his response.

"It was a legal shoot," he said.

"I'm sure it was. Thanks for the information."

"Does that help somehow? Who cares how we tracked them?"

Sam shrugged. "I got no idea what matters yet. I don't know. You can't put a puzzle together unless you got all the pieces. And knowing about how you found 'em, what led you to them, well, that's a piece of it."

Sheriff Douglas drank his drink and started out, pausing at the doorway and turning back.

"Well, Sam Colder, it sounds to me like you intend to make something that is real simple into something complicated. Some bandits killed people, and we caught them."

"And I ain't saying that ain't exactly right," Sam said. "And I got no problem with it being complicated or simple. Either way suits me as long as it gets to the truth."

"Hope that don't bite you on the ass," Douglas said.

Then he walked out.

Redding took out a handkerchief and wiped his brow. "I'm heading home now, but I'll draw you a map to the place and the Chancellor and Evert Ranches and have it for you in the morning," he said.

"And the Holloway homestead," Sam said.

"Fine. But it will take you some time to cover that much ground. Days. And for nothing."

"Seeing as I came this far, I might as well do things right."

The mayor scowled at Donna. "You coming?"

She shook her head. "Emily is in back fixing dinner. I got me a customer and need to get him settled in his room. I'll have Emily bring you your supper when it's ready."

"And you?"

"I'll be home when I'm done here, Elmore Redding, and not a moment sooner."

When he left, Donna grinned. "Well, it's just you and me now," she said. "Another goddamn quiet night in Rock Canyon."

"And that's normal?"

She winked. "Friday nights are sometimes a bit crazy. Why, we can have five or six people come in for drinks on a night like that."

She led him out back to where two small, squat adobe structures sat. "Either one is yours," she said.

He picked one at random and found it was a tiny square room with a bed, a dresser, and a window that had a view of the whitewashed adobe wall of the next building.

"They ain't much," she said.

They weren't.

Tossing his saddlebags on the bed, Sam nodded. "It'll do."

They went back to the saloon. He sat at a table, easing into a cane-bottomed chair. Donna sat with him.

"And you work here when the ranch hands come in here looking for a good time?"

She laughed. "Emily works for us at the house and the saloon. When we got some customers, I tend bar and she serves drinks."

"And the mayor is good with that?"

"You mean me being around a bunch of horny cowboys?" She laughed. "Anything beyond drinks and dinner, well, that's between them and Emily."

Maybe yes, maybe no. Donna's flirting made it unclear how true that was.

She refilled his glass, then sat the bottle on the bar. As she released it, her fingers touched his arm.

"I'll go check on the stew and have her make up some fry bread."

"Sounds good. I'm starving."

Watching her wiggle her ass for him as she headed into the cooking area, he was sure that stew, bread, and whisky weren't the only items on the menu.

When another girl came in carrying the food, Donna introduced her as Emily.

The thin girl of indeterminate age, with lifeless hair and dull eyes was a child of defeat. He'd seen a number like her, who had parted company with any kind of hope a long time ago.

"Em is a good help around here," she said.

"Everyone needs good help," he said.

"I'm going to have to get home to Elmore. He'll be expecting me. The town is dead, so Emily will hang around until you are ready to go to bed. She can get you drinks and whatever."

She smiled as she said 'whatever.'

"Fine."

As the girl puttered, Donna put a hand on his arm. "As I said, if you are of a mind to, the girl will fuck you any way you want for a couple of dollars."

"Not tonight," he said.

Memories of Victoria would hold him over for a time.

She nodded. "Sometimes it's good to hold out for something better," she said.

Then she left.

Sam finished his drink, had the girl refill his glass, and then said good night. Leaving, he had no idea if the girl cared one way or the other that he hadn't asked her to come to his room, and he was just as glad.

Chapter 8

Jubal Holloway

It was cool when Sam got up, just before dawn. An orange light was starting to dance along the ragged tops of the mountain ridges in the distance. Day was coming and even though Rock Canyon was at seven thousand feet, and the altitude kept things cooler, you could feel that it would be hot soon.

The tableland downhill a couple thousand feet would be even hotter. Oven hot. And later, when he'd finished up a few things, that lower, hot land was where he'd be heading. But now he had to get the map that Redding had promised, and he wanted to talk to Douglas' prisoners.

He owed those men a chance to explain their story, even though, knowing Douglas, he doubted he'd learn much from them that was real.

From what Redding had said, it seemed he'd need to cover some distance, so he'd need to replenish his supplies. He needed some beans and dried meat, and, in case there was trouble, another box of ammo might be useful. It struck him as just good sense to expect more trouble. Someone certainly hadn't wanted him here in the first place.

In the saloon, Emily provided him with a good breakfast, giving him her blank, detached, stare. She was pleasant enough but never seemed entirely there. It was like her thoughts were somewhere else, as if she was stuck in some more pleasant past that she didn't want to leave. Or perhaps she was woolgathering about a fantasy future?

He couldn't know, and she didn't seem inclined to say anything that she didn't have to say. But he guessed that at some point the world she lived in bothered her enough that she preferred staying in her head and living somewhere else.

Sam couldn't understand how a person could live that way, imagining better times and places and not doing anything to get to them. But then, he knew nothing about her and didn't have a clue what made her that way. The end result was that she appeared to live each day without really experiencing it.

That made being around her bittersweet. A woman like that was living life almost invisible—a sad soul who stood still marking time in a world that moved around her.

Of course, Rock Canyon offered her nothing... no social life beyond her work and her employers, and the handful of other employees. It had to be hard to have dreams in that world.

And maybe there were more people like that in the world than he ever knew—going through the motions of life. Maybe others hid it better or expressed it differently. How would you know unless you looked for them?

As he finished his coffee, an intense young man came into the bar. Long and lean, his bones pronounced, he had yellow hair, a scruffy pretense of a mustache, and he wore the clothes of a working man.

After a glance around, the man made a bee-line for Sam's table. Stopping in front of him, the young man pulled off his hat and ran his fingers through his hair. "You're Mr. Colder? Sam Colder?"

"That's right," he said.

"I'm Jubal Holloway," he said. "I need to talk with you."

"Sit," Sam said, indicating the empty chair across from him. "I was planning on coming out to see you. Seems you saved me a trip."

"You wanted to talk to me? I figured the governor was just ignoring me."

"Judge March said he sent you a telegram."

A look of surprise crossed the young man's face. "Well, the telegraph operator works for the mayor, and he weren't too thrilled at me contacting Prescott. I even went to Nogales to send the telegram to him because I thought it might somehow get lost if I sent it here." He grinned. "Guess I wasn't imagining things."

"I guess you weren't," Sam agreed. "How did you know my name?"

Jubal smiled. "Even the mayor and his pet sheriff can't stop gossip."

He turned to Emily. "Em, get this young man a cup of coffee."

Jubal smiled his thanks. "And you are here to investigate? Have you learned anything?"

Sam pursed his lips. "I just got into town last night. All I know is that the sheriff has a couple of Mexicans in custody. He thinks they did the killing."

Jubal glanced around as if he wanted to see who might be listening in. "From the beginning, Mayor Redding said it was Mexican bandits, and he hired that asshole Douglas to prove it."

"So you don't think—"

"None of the homesteaders think it was Mexicans," he said.

"Well, I'm going to talk with the prisoners myself and see what they got to say."

"He is just stalling for time."

"Why? If the truth comes out, then it does."

"Look, people are scared. Chancellor and his men have them thinking that if they got innocent men in jail, then there ain't no reason for the governor to send help."

"And yet, here I am."

"But you can't stop raids all by yourself. At least they'll think that."

"If you are right, what good does that do the ranchers?"

Jubal licked his lips as Emily sat the coffee in front of him and flashed her a smile that disappeared into her dullness.

"Look, if they scare people off, that's all they need or want. When homesteaders leave a property, whether they give up and go somewhere else, or are driven off, or die, the land goes back to the government. That means the ranchers can tear down any fences and go back to grazing their cattle on it. You might have noticed that grass is a tad sparse out here."

"I had noticed that," Sam said.

"It takes a lot of acreage to fatten a cow, and each homestead takes away at least one hundred and sixty acres of grazing land. But, if something bad happens to the homesteaders, that turns back the clock for the ranchers. Gives them free land."

"Are the scare tactics working?"

"Sure. There ain't many of us and the homesteads are scattered about. And since homesteaders don't have money, the politicians don't give them much thought."

"Then you think the ranchers have someone killing them so that their land is available for grazing?"

"All I know is that no one has seen any bandits around for ages. After the massacres started, the mayor claimed they were doing it. Then John Chancellor hired Sheriff Douglas."

"Not the mayor?"

"The mayor might as well work for Chancellor. And he pays the sheriff's salary out of his pocket. That makes me think he might be inclined to find some Mexican bandits guilty of the crime while the real criminals get on with business. This is the time of year that the ranchers need to fatten the cattle up."

"Indeed it is. But you are going to fight back?"

"I got married recently, just before we came out here. Me and Charity, that's my wife, we put everything we had into this homestead. If we fail, we got nowhere to go," he said, looking embarrassed.

They'd made a hell of a gamble on an uncertain future.

"So Chancellor is your concern? You think he might be behind the massacres, and bandits and Indians got nothing to do with it."

"Mostly. That's what it sure seems like."

"What about other ranchers?"

"Evert is the only other one big enough and rich enough to pay people to do such things. Now he hates homesteaders, but not as people. He hates seeing us putting up fences and he hates seeing the grassland plowed up, but he knows it ain't his land. I've talked to him, and he grudgingly accepts that we are trying to earn a living, same as him."

"Good to know. I'll talk to him, anyway."

"How will you find out the truth?"

"That's a damn good question," Sam said. "An investigation is a lot like hunting. It requires digging around and seeing what you might startle, bring out of hiding. So I'll be poking my nose into lotsa things and then I'll follow whatever scoots out and see where it goes."

"And in the meantime..."

"Be alert. If we are lucky, I'll find out that the sheriff has the right culprits. If he's wrong, or someone is fooling us, then we can hope the real villains will keep a lid on things for a time."

"Why would they do that? Everyone is scared now. They might push ahead."

"Well, if they are framing these Mexicans, the only reason to do that is to keep the governor from deciding that things are out of their control. They don't want him sending troops out here to provide protection for the citizens."

"I guess not."

"More attacks would show they got it wrong. So, if they play it smart, then we will have the time to unravel whatever is going on before it blows up."

As Emily put a coffee in front of him, Jubal sighed.

"What if they don't play it smart? What if they decide you might see through their game?"

Sam gave the boy a hard look but spoke kindly. "Then I reckon we best hope they do something stupid that tips their hand before they hurt more folks."

"I don't want to see more people hurt," Jubal said.

Especially a young woman named Charity, Sam was certain.

"Me either," he said. "I'm not wasting any time, son. You can believe that."

"If anything happens…"

The young man let the statement hang. He didn't need to finish it. Many of the homesteaders probably were backed into a corner by similar circumstances, and desperation made a man think of doing terrible things.

"You go home and do your work, keep your family safe while I investigate, and I'll do everything I can to get at the truth," Sam said.

Jubal stood and held out a hand.

"I'll take your word on that, Mister Colder."

The handshake was firm and honest.

"You've got it, Mister Holloway."

From where Sam sat, a man like Jubal Holloway would have a rough time. But the west could do with a lot more idealistic people just like him.

Chapter 9

Confessions

The two Mexicans were brothers, they told him. Hector and Flacco Rodriguez. They were from the area.

The rest of the story was exactly what Douglas had told him. When they were arrested, they'd been camping up on the ridge above the town, they told him. Their friend, Carlos, went for his gun and the sheriff shot him. Hector and Flacco surrendered.

The marks on their faces and bodies suggested that each had been beaten in a rather methodical manner, yet the men claimed they'd fought back when the sheriff and deputy arrived and suffered their injuries in the scuffle.

After they surrendered? Sam doubted it but this wasn't the time to point out the inconsistencies.

More to the point, they confessed, almost eagerly, to being the raiders who had killed the homesteaders.

"Why?" he asked them.

"For money and food," Hector said.

"And their guns," Flacco said. "We fight the Apache often, and it takes weapons to drive away los Indios."

That, at least, made a certain amount of sense. The Chiricahua definitely fought the Mexicans along this part of the border, and some stealing might have fit the story, but these two were soft. Their eyes were those of farmers, not ruthless gunmen. Not killers.

And they were terrified. Whatever Douglas had threatened them with made them stick to their story like religious converts. And it wasn't a fear of being beaten more, or killed. No, this went deeper. Douglas had some big stick and had used it to convince them to tell the story he wanted Sam to hear.

Much to Douglas' disgust, he insisted on having the men separated and then asked them individually to repeat their stories.

They were identical. They weren't telling what happened, just repeating something they'd been told to say.

Seemed likely they'd say it the same way in front of a judge, too.

Getting at the truth of this matter would mean learning more about the men... who they were. At least it would help to know more.

"Satisfied?" Douglas asked him, not trying to hide his sneer of contempt.

"What are you asking?" Sam asked him.

"You heard their confessions and I'm asking if now you'll tell the big shots in the capitol that we got the right men in jail, that we are doing our job."

"I've listened to them. I also noticed that they got beaten pretty bad," Sam said. "Men say a lot of things when they've been hurt and promised more hurt if they don't play along."

Sheriff Douglas bristled. "You think we convinced them to confess to a hanging offense by treating them a little rough?"

"Not exactly," Sam said. "But I have other people to talk to."

"Do you now? Like who?"

"The ranchers in the area, some of their hands."

"I talked to them already," Douglas said.

"I'm sure you did. But like with these men, I want to hear their side of things myself. There seem to be several things going on around here."

"You are a troublemaker, Colder."

Sam leveled his gaze at the man and took in the anger building up in him. That was fine, it would keep him off balance.

"If me doing my job, investigating the troubles here makes trouble for you, then maybe you got something to worry about."

"Well, it don't. You're just a pain."

"One other thing," Sam said. "I took note of the cuts and bruises on those men. When I get back to town, I'll need to talk to them again. I best not see any new marks. They better be recovering from their injuries or not getting worse."

Douglas gave him a defiant glare. "You wor‐ried about your Mexicans?"

"While they are in your custody, I am."

"What do you intend to do if I rough them up?"

"Ask the governor to authorize your arrest and take you to Prescott to stand trial," Sam said.

"Shit."

On the walk back to the saloon, Sam cursed himself for letting Douglas get to him. In his anger, he'd said more than he should have. It wasn't good to make Douglas think he doubt‐ed the frame that much. It was fine to have doubts, but taking the side of the prisoners had been too much.

In the saloon, he sat down and asked Emily to bring him a drink.

"You talk to those Mexicans?" she asked him.

"I did."

"You think they did it?"

Something in her voice touched him and made him want to answer what sounded like an honest question. And this was the most the woman had ever spoken to him.

"I don't think they did. I think he managed to scare them into confessing."

She nodded and wandered behind the bar, holding a rag and listlessly wiping the surface.

Donna came in and sat at his table. "Emily said you were needing supplies for your trip," she said. "Give me a list and I'd be glad to have her get them things from the store for you."

"That'd be right nice," he said. He'd entirely forgotten about the shopping, and when Emily came over with a piece of paper and pencil, he wrote down what he needed. Then the girl took it and went to the store.

"You gonna talk to the Chancellors and the Everts?" Donna asked.

"That's what I had in mind. I want to look at the massacre locations, too."

She handed him a map. Elmore drew it out. He's pretty good with drawing and gets the scale pretty nice."

It was a decent map, and it referenced Rock Canyon and the nearby mountains, with an "x" indicating each ranch, the Holloway place, and the two most recent massacres.

It was, as the mayor had said, a fair piece of ground to cover.

"The best route would be to go see the Chancellors first," she said, pointing. It's only half a day away."

That looked about right. Half a day, a blazing afternoon ride over sunbaked hard-packed sand under a cloudless sky.

"I'll see," he said.

He had no interest in telling anyone his route. But a little test could be in order.

He pointed on the map. "On the way in, it seemed to me that there might be a nice place to camp over by where this homestead used to be."

She nodded. "Chancellors would probably offer you dinner and a soft bed."

"I'll consider that as a good possibility," he said.

She got up. "Suit yourself."

As she went behind the bar and began taking inventory of the bottles on the shelves behind it, Sam turned back to his thoughts until Emily came in with a box holding the things on his list. She put it on the table.

"I'll refill that glass," she said, going to the bar and returning with the bottle. Her back was to Donna, and as she poured the whisky, she stuffed a piece of paper into his shirt pocket.

"I think I got everything on your list, but you best double check. Especially the things on the back."

"I didn't—"

He glanced up and saw the warning on her face.

Taking the paper out, he looked at his list, then turned it over and saw a map. It showed a location that appeared to be further out than the homestead massacres. It gave a few landmarks, and a circle marked a location where she'd written the name "Rodriguez."

The same name as the prisoners.

At the bottom, she had written, in a childish scrawl: "If you truly want answers."

"Thank you," he said, looking in the box as if he was checking it. "That's a big help, Emily."

Donna looked up. "Thank you, Donna. I best get going."

"I'll put them things on your tab," she said.

"Perfect." He smiled his thanks at Emily, and she walked away.

The tiny town of Rock Canyon was turning out to be filled with surprises.

Chapter 10

Hardscrabble

Two days of steady riding from Rock Canyon brought Sam to a hardscrabble farm that sat low on the flat land. It was stuck in the middle of nowhere.

It made Sam's heart ache to think of people trying to make a living by farming this land. Just staying even in that struggle, keeping ahead of starvation, was going to be difficult at best. When people didn't leave you alone, much less offer help, the odds stacked up against you fast.

A few chickens kicked up dust around a small, windowless adobe house. A burro, obviously used for hauling water from who knew where, stood in the shade of a collapsing shed next to the house. Raggedy fences of chicken wire enclosed a small vegetable garden that was the only color he could see.

He rode up slowly and as he approached, a Mexican woman came out, holding a carbine.

"Hola," he called out in his friendliest voice.

The lady wasn't buying his pitch. She pointed the gun at him.

"Salir de aquí ahora," she said.

Her tone of voice made the message clear. He would have understood her even if he didn't speak two words of Spanish. She wanted him off her property.

He switched his brain into his best Spanish. "I've just seen Hector and Flacco," he said.

The hardness in her face intensified. "You come to tell me those men killed them?"

"No, Señora. They are very much alive. The sheriff has them in jail, and they were beaten, but they are alive."

"Then why are you here?"

"To learn the truth."

She laughed.

"Why did the sheriff arrest them?" Sam asked.

"Arrest them?" She laughed. "That was not an arrest. Five men came riding in one night. We were eating, and they came in. One man shot Carlos and they beat the other men. If that was an arrest, their crime was being Mexican."

"And the sheriff took them away."

"Eventually," her face twisted with hate.

"Did they say anything?"

"Just that our men were bandits and that if we, their women, showed our faces in the pueblo of *cañón de roca*, they would kill us."

She spat. "As if we were ever welcome in that pueblo, anyway."

Cañón de roca was Spanish for Rock canyon. And Sheriff Douglas had clearly omitted a few details from his arrest report.

"They gave no reason for suspecting your men?"

"Them being filthy Mexicans was the only reason they gave." She spat on the ground. "Those hombres didn't seem to find Mexican women quite so filthy. At least not so filthy that they weren't happy to take turns fucking us. Not even when the filthy women screamed for them to leave them alone."

It was hard to hear, but with men like that… the men raping them could hardly be a surprise. They took whatever they wanted, and it wasn't like anyone could stand up for these women.

She let the barrel of the rifle drop. "And you say they have not killed them?"

"Hector and Flacco were alive when I left. The mayor had them bury the other man — Carlos."

The woman crossed herself, and Sam heard a wailing come from the house.

"His wife," she said. "When they took him away, she didn't know if he was dead or not. She grieves, but the comfort of knowing his fate will let it pass."

"I see."

"And you rode all this way to tell us this?"

"No," he said. "The sheriff forced them to confess to some killings... of homesteaders."

"Those massacres!" She shook her head. "The men who came here were doing the killing, not our men."

"You know this for certain? It couldn't have been Indians?"

She nodded firmly. "Consuela, my sister, who is Flacco's wife, was working for one of the families. The wife took sick, and they hired her to do the cooking and taking care of the children."

"Which family?"

She pointed north. "The Walkers."

They were the most recent.

"One noche, one night, she left their homestead to come home. She was a small distance from the house, walking in the dark, when five blancos rode in screaming and shooting. She hid in the hills, afraid to move. They slaughtered the family and set fire to the buildings."

That matched the information he had.

"And the sheriff claims that our men were the ones who killed those people!"

"He does."

"What can we do?" she asked.

"I'm doing everything I can to prove they are innocent," he said.

She clucked her tongue. "Then they will kill you."

"They might try," he said.

"They are bad men. No one can stop them," she said.

"Three of them tried to kill me already. And two of them are dead for their trouble. The third might be as well. He rode away with a bullet in him."

"God forgive me, but I am glad to hear that," she said.

"Then perhaps in a few days, I might be able to give you more good news."

"I will pray you are successful," she said, crossing herself. "We will all pray for you and this good work you are doing."

"How are you for food?" he asked.

She smiled thinly. "As usual," she said. "With fewer mouths to feed and fewer hands to find food, God balances things."

He unhooked the two rabbits he had trapped from the pommel of his saddle.

"I can offer you these and a few cans of things."

"And what will you eat?" she asked.

"I don't need much," he said. "And there is more game in the hills."

She snorted. "You should save your energy and time for killing that bastard who is the sheriff. And for now, we will accept your gift on the condition that you eat with us."

Sam smiled. "Señora, that is the kindest, most welcoming offer I've gotten since I arrived in Rock Canyon."

Walking over to take the rabbits, she pointed at the shed. "Then put your horse in the shade and unsaddle him, then come in."

You made friends where you could in this world and Sam felt he had a chance to make some here. And if he could make friends by doing the right thing, that would please him even more.

Chapter 11

The Chancellors

Amy Chancellor was tall, regal, and somewhat fierce looking. If she smiled, it might make her face attractive, but smiling didn't come naturally to her.

Watching her as she invited him into her house, the confident way she moved, made him think she was probably as good a rider, and maybe even as good a shot, as any man. Some women didn't belong on a ranch, or only belonged there if they had the right support, but Amy Chancellor was at home there in every important way.

As she led him into a cool courtyard, a petite Mexican girl dressed in a brightly colored floral print dress scurried up to them. "Señora?"

"Send for my husband, then bring Mister Colder a mescal," Amy Chancellor said as she pointed to a table and chairs sitting under the shade of a tree.

When he sat, she took the seat opposite him, her hands folded in her lap. Something about her face seemed familiar. Not that he'd met her before, just that she reminded him of someone.

She grinned at him. "You are trying to figure out why you think you should know me," she said.

"Something like that," he admitted.

"Donna Redding is my little sister. We don't look as much alike as we did when we was younger, but the family resemblance is strong."

"Yes, it is."

"Now tell me why you'd ride all the way out here to talk with us."

"It's about the massacres," he said, noting her flinching slightly at the word.

"The killings…, yes, we heard the government was sending someone to investigate," she said. "I should have assumed that whoever the governor sent might want to chat with all the ranchers."

Sam looked around, giving himself a moment to collect his thoughts, but also to admire the house. The ranch house, the hacienda, had been built in a Spanish style, with adobe walls and a roof of curved red tiles. In the center, protected from the wind, was this courtyard, which was covered with large, flat stones and filled with green plants in bright Mexican pottery.

It had been a lot of work, but well worth it. They had good taste in architecture.

When the girl brought his drink, he smiled his thanks. The ceramic goblet was cool to the touch.

Sam looked into her large, brown eyes and saw her return the smile before backing away and leaving him to sit back, sipping the mescal. A place like this, away from the bullshit of town, was nice. He could do without the ranch, but a house like this could make living in the high desert pleasant, even comfortable.

"I guess the news gets around fast, even out here," he said.

"The news you were coming, but nothing about what all these killings might have to do with us. We don't know anything that might help you."

If she wanted to help him.

"I have no idea," Sam said. "But if you thought I'd naturally come to see you, maybe you have an idea of your own."

"Not really," she said. Then she laughed. "Well, I'll admit I gave some thought to the politics of the matter."

"The politics?"

"The governor is going to hear from the homesteaders that we don't want them here. Of course, we don't, but that is out of our hands."

"Unless the homesteaders are somehow convinced to leave before their two years of homesteading is up."

"Five years," she said with a smile. "Under the 1862 act."

"You would know better than I."

"So, the governor might think, or be convinced to think, that these poor people being murdered, these massacres around rock canyon have something to do with us. That we were trying to kill them off, chase off the rest." She scowled. "Of course, that is nonsense."

"Not an unreasonable thing for him to consider," Sam said. "You ranchers have a lot of clout, but with civilization coming to the territory, there is a lot of talk about people's rights and the liberties some folk take. There's even talk of giving women the vote."

She snorted. "As if we need a vote."

"Well, I don't know if you've heard this news, but the sheriff in Rock Canyon arrested some Mexicans. He says they are part of a bandit gang."

"I did hear that," she said. "Good for him. Doesn't that settle things?"

Sam sighed. "He got them to confess."

"Well, then... that's the end of that dreadful speculation."

Sam raised an eyebrow. "Maybe. Might be."

"Why would you doubt they massacred those people?"

He'd gotten her attention and now she was fishing, trying to get a handle on his thinking. The dumb cowboy the government sent was playing his cards close to his vest and she didn't much like that.

"I got no idea for certain. The problem is that I need more than his hunch."

"They confessed, you said. Surely that wraps it up."

"Not entirely. He's got some half-assed confessions that he and his deputy beat out of those men and taught them to repeat on cue, using English words they don't even understand."

"Why would he do that?"

"Well, he's a lawman. Catching the culprits makes him look good. This way, even if there are more incidents, he can say he only got part of a bigger gang."

"And you think it was someone else?"

"Maybe. My problem is that the governor sent me out to find out what is going on. Not just grab the first answer that's handed to me on a platter. You see, if the sheriff is wrong and I don't work out who is doing it, then we still got bad men out there. They might kill other homesteaders, or they might get brave and decide a rancho, a place like this, would be a juicier target."

"Now I think you are just trying to scare me," she said. "Why do you want to do that?"

She didn't look in the least frightened. Actually, she looked rather regal. Whether that was because the bandits didn't really worry her, or because she had nothing to worry about was hard to tell.

"Not trying to do that at all, Mrs. Chancellor. Just speaking the truth as I see it."

"We aren't in danger. We have ranch hands here. Men who will defend the place."

"And that's one reason I'm here."

She laughed. "Are you looking for protection, Mr. Colder?"

"Your hands got eyes and ears. Their chores take them all over the ranch and the grazing land, including where homesteads are. I thought they might have seen something."

"We would have told the sheriff if they had," she snapped.

"If the hands told you," Sam said.

That caught her by surprise. "Why wouldn't they?"

"Lots of cowboys don't want to get involved in shit like that—killings. Some of the men are probably wanted men themselves."

"We wouldn't hire—"

"It ain't likely they'd mention it. But working a ranch keeps them out of sight for a time. And there are lots of other reasons they might not mention seeing a bunch of Mexicans riding away from a homestead, or headed toward one." He winked. "If they did, that would support the sheriff's theory."

"Theory? Dead people aren't a theory."

"The theory is about who did it. And even the sheriff can't explain why these boys would do it. There ain't no money in robbing homesteaders."

"You are talking about vicious, filthy Mexicans," she said, echoing the words he'd heard from the Rodriguez family. The hardening of her face told him she had no love for Mexicans.

When he arrived, John Chancellor, her husband, wasn't any more helpful. An older man, toughened by his years of ranching the harsh land, he saw things in a version of black and white that was tilted toward his own experiences and upbringing.

"I figured you'd want to know what the hands might have seen," he said when he joined them.

The Mexican girl, invisible to them, brought him a glass of cool mescal.

"I asked the boys if they have seen anything unusual, anything that might get them thinking," Chancellor said. "They ain't seen nothing worth talking about."

"Mr. Colder was hoping they could help him because he doesn't think it was that Mexicans did it," Amy Chancellor said.

"Then who the fuck do you think did it?" John Chancellor asked.

Sam spread his hands out.

"That's what I'm trying to determine. And your wife is putting words in my mouth."

"You said the sheriff just had a theory."

"I also said the sheriff might be right." He pointed at John Chancellor. "I understand you are paying the sheriff's salary."

The man sat upright. "Maria! Another mescal," he said.

He sat, stewing until the girl refilled his glass.

"Yes, I agreed to pay it. Elmore and I got into it about the old sheriff. He was a worthless piece of shit. I met this man, and he was looking for a job. He promised some results but wanted more money. That made Elmore choke, but he seemed able to handle himself, so I agreed to pay his salary."

"Did you know he was an outlaw?"

Chancellor nodded. "He told me. Takes one to know one, I figure. And it seems he got results in pretty short order."

"He did."

The man scowled. "And yet, here you are, looking to prove he didn't get the killers."

"I'm looking for another theory, is more like it."

"Theory?"

"See, the problem is, even if he has the killers in jail, even if these Mexicans did the killing, I don't think it was just a raid. There ain't no money in it for them."

Chancellor's eyes brightened. "Then you think someone paid them to kill those people?"

"I didn't say I thought they killed those people. But if they did, there was more to it than just a raid. That worries me, because then whoever paid them can just hire more men, better killers."

"Well, them homesteaders do make themselves easy targets, even for a bumbling Mexican. A handful of squatters spread out across open range—just a man and his woman with maybe a kid or two trying to make a go of it on one hundred and sixty acres of land... hell, you can't defend a place with so few people. Bandits, Indians, and just cowboys drunk on cheap whisky are all threats to them. It's a risky life. Getting all worked up over a few deaths, calling them massacres, that's just nuts."

"So what should those people do?"

He snorted. "Move into town. If they are worried about dying, that'll do it. Or maybe they should head back east where it's safe."

"You think they'd be safe back east?" Sam asked.

"Ain't no marauding Mexicans there, at least."

That might be true.

"You aren't thrilled with them being out there."

"They don't belong there," he said.

"The Federal Government gave them the land. It's theirs if they work it. So where else do they belong?"

"Giveaways like that are bull crap. If a man can't hold onto his land himself, if he needs the government to hold it for him, he don't belong there."

And that was the end of the conversation.

Now that Chancellor had stated his judgment on the homesteaders out loud, Sam wasn't going to get any more information. Opinions, maybe.

And that got him wanting to poke the bear in his den.

Standing, he said goodbye and thanked them for their hospitality. Then, as they walked him to the door, he turned to face John Chancellor.

"I get the impression that the killings of the homesteaders don't make you unhappy in the least, Mr. Chancellor. Is that a fair statement?"

Chancellor's neck turned red. "You implying something, Mr. Colder?"

"No, Mr. Chancellor. I'm asking a question on behalf of the governor."

"Well, you can tell that asshole in Prescott exactly what I said, that them people don't belong out here. I'm not happy they got killed, but it wouldn't sadden my heart if they all left. The land should stay wild."

"Cattle grazing on it ain't exactly wild," Sam said. "That's why you hunt the wolves, to make it safe for animals that don't belong out there."

"It belongs to the animals who feed on it and the men who care for them."

Getting on Rocky, Sam struggled to understand a man like John Chancellor.

The fact that he'd succeeded out here suggested he was a hard worker, and while Sam didn't like him much, he seemed honest. The man certainly didn't like the homesteaders much, and might not lift a finger to help them, but Sam couldn't bring himself to believe that the man ordered their murders.

But that didn't mean he hadn't.

"Are you heading back to town, or will you talk to the Evert's place first?" Amy Chancellor asked.

Her assumption, or knowledge, amused him. She didn't mind him knowing that she was on top of everything going on in her domain.

"I already chatted with them earlier," he said. "I'm going to go straight back from here and see if there is any news."

The visit to the other ranch hadn't been any more helpful than this one. Not directly, at least. The Evert family had a smaller ranch than the one the Chancellors commanded, but their greed was just as big. Like Chancellor, they were sure that as ranchers, early settlers in the area, their time here in the territory entitled them to have the land available for their cattle.

"We been here for generations," Evert told him. "Them cattle need to range as far as the eye can see, and we fought Indians and bandits to make sure they could. Now it seems like we gotta fight the federal government, too."

And that was a way of looking at it. Certainly, the encroachment of civilization disrupted and changed the lives of the early frontiersmen, just as their encroachment had disrupted the lives of the Indians and the Spanish.

Now, as he settled in his saddle, Amy Chancellor walked up to stroke Rocky's nose. Her hand touched the hackamore and she smiled appreciatively at the horse, the way a serious horsewoman would.

"Mr. Colder, would you mind delivering a message for us?"

"Depends on what it is," he said. "One if by land? Something like that?"

"Nothing so... revolutionary," she joked. "We'd like you to tell Mayor Redding that John and I would like to see him out here at his earliest convenience? We would like to talk some business and will put him up for a couple of nights."

"I can pass that along for you," Sam said.

"Tell him it's about a large order we are going to need to make."

"That should motivate the man," Sam said.

"Ride safe," she said.

Chapter 12

What Did You Learn?

Sam rode into Rock Canyon feeling fresh and alert. He'd spent the night camped at the edge of town. Perched on an outcropping that gave him a view of anyone coming and going, he'd spent a restful night, putting the claims and counterclaims about the massacres out of his head.

Now, as the morning light had begun to color the sky, painting the hills a deep red, he came into town.

The town was quiet, but already the situation was in his head again, churning over. Whatever was going on was twisted in many unpleasant ways. In a place with few people, there was more than enough mistrust and dislike to go around.

Yet, a few things seemed clear. The Mexicans Douglas had in jail weren't bandits. Talking to them, seeing how they'd been treated, made that clear as the afternoon sky would be. He wouldn't have left them in that jail, under Mark Douglas's care, except that it gave him some cover. With the entire town and the countryside watching his every move, he needed to keep whoever was pulling the strings to feel off balance. That had meant letting them think he was willing to consider the hapless Mexican farmers as suspects while he learned more.

But he didn't want them feeling too safe, either. He needed them to act.

Unfortunately, their actions so far had resulted in a lot of deaths, and he didn't want to provoke more killing. He had to walk a narrow trail of keeping them guessing, but not quite panicked.

Over the years, he'd learned that when you got to walk an unfamiliar trail barefoot and blindfolded, the way he was now, it was best to do it rested. So, he woke early and found he was ready to stir the pot a little, to make things happen.

Sam didn't much care for the town of Rock Canyon, or its people, and finishing the job up as quick as possible suited him. With any luck, he could figure it all out, send off a telegram, and then head to Nogales. Heading that way, he might catch up with Doc Johnson's medicine show and have a chance to savor another delicious taste of exotic dancing.

Or he could head right back to Prescott, stopping at Tucson along the way. Both cities offered many delights there for the taking.

That was a tempting option, as Thelma had promised him a bonus for doing this job and he was curious to find out what she had in mind.

Either way, waiting for things to happen wasn't in the cards. The brains and money behind the killings could easily wait him out. They were in a bit of a rush, but time was more their friend than his.

Mayor Redding came clattering down the stairs from his office even before Sam hitched Rocky to the pole on the ramada.

"You got back sooner than I thought," he said.

"Well, I managed to take care of one interview before I even left," he said.

"Holloway," the mayor said, making no effort to hide his disgust. Then he brightened. "Did you find the answers you were looking for?"

"Not hardly," Sam told him. "But I got a lot of the information the governor wanted."

"Information?"

"Things he wanted to know about."

"Like what?"

"I'll be reporting it to him. I can't really say more than that."

That didn't please Elmore Redding, who clearly wanted details and seemed to think he deserved them.

"Well, soon as you are ready, let me know. I'll my clerk send a telegram for you."

Sam smiled. "That's a right nice offer. I might take you up on it, but just to let the people in Prescott know that I'm still investigating."

"You won't update them?"

Sam shook his head. "I'm not so good with writing things out. I let them know that when I took the job. Besides, I promised I'd deliver my report in person. That way, there won't be no misunderstandings. They might have questions about the bandits you caught, for instance, and I'll be right there to answer them."

"So you are done with your investigation, then?" The man couldn't hide his hope.

"Not even close," he said. "Got to keep poking around until things get more clear."

As Redding's face fell, Sam slapped his arm.

"Well, I got some news for you, personally. The Chancellors asked me to give you a message, Mister Mayor. As soon as you can arrange it, they'd like you to head out to their place for a couple of days to talk about some business."

"Business?"

"Some order or other. They want you out there as their guest for a couple of days. Sounds like you'll get to stay in that lovely hacienda. While sitting in the courtyard is about as much of their hospitality as I've sampled, I'm willing to bet the food will be real fine."

The thought seemed to please him. He smiled as he considered it.

"Might be real nice to slip away for a time, get out of this town for a couple of days at that," he said. "Get away from the pressures."

Sam wondered what pressures the man thought he faced. Not that it was worth asking.

"I'm sure your wife and your people can manage without you for that long," Sam said.

Elmore Redding was a vain fool, and pretty useless. Sam was sure that he was a convenient tool for the ranchers under normal circumstances. Now, there was a reason that Amy Chancellor had sent for him, and he doubted that the business she'd mentioned had much to do with it. More likely, it had something to do with his investigation... leading him in a new direction or stopping him altogether.

Seeing what it was would prove interesting. Amy and John Chancellor were tough, no-nonsense people. Pragmatic in the way that frontier people had to be. For all he knew, this message was to get Redding, who might not have the stomach for the hard plays, out of the way so their other hired hand, Mark Douglas, could do a job. It well might be that Sam was the task that needed tending to.

The Mark Douglas he knew was a shifty man and didn't give a shit about much but himself. He figured to be loyal to whoever was paying him, as long as they were paying him, and until he got a better offer.

If Douglas was the same person, and he seemed like it, being asked to kill a man would just be another job he had to do, among others. With Sam questioning things, challenging the story the good people of Rock Canyon had created, he had no doubt that whoever was behind the murders of the homesteaders probably had arranged his ambush, and now would at least have seriously considered the possibility of having him killed right there in town.

That would make sense to her if she wanted to slow down the investigation and have time to work more on getting rid of the homesteaders.

And no one in Prescott would ever know they'd have him killed. They would hear that he disappeared out in the desert on one of his investigative trips. They'd suggest logical stories, that maybe he had cornered the rest of the Mexican bandit gang, for instance, but bit off more than he could chew.

Shit like that happened out here. And with the distance between Rock Canyon and Prescott, the governor's office wouldn't be able to learn the truth about what happened easily.

So he could expect things to get interesting over the next couple of days. He'd pay extra attention. Still, whether he came out on top or not... well, like everyone else, he'd have to wait and see.

The town seemed unnaturally quiet after Elmore Redding set off for his in-laws' place. But, as he'd been told, the few residents were holed up in the buildings, working. Except on paydays, there wasn't any social activity. People didn't seem to stroll, or even step outside for a smoke very often.

A strange place.

"Is this town quieter than normal?" he asked Emily as she puttered behind the bar.

She gave him a startled look.

"You asking me?"

"Sure. Ain't no one else here."

She shrugged. "I guess it might be."

"Any reason for it?"

"It's a small town," she said. "A couple of people, like the mayor leave and it seems quieter. And I know Tank, the deputy went out looking for raiders."

"Really?"

"The missus said he'll be gone all night and I'm supposed to take the sheriff his dinner over at the jail cause he don't want the prisoners left unattended."

That news didn't sadden Sam's heart in the slightest. He'd do right fine with one less enemy to watch for. It got tiring watching your back. If Tank left and the sheriff was keeping guard, he didn't have to wonder if one of them would pop into the saloon at any moment.

He was even more sure he would do fine with this town being quiet when Donna wandered in and invited him to have dinner with her at her house.

"I don't like eating alone," she said. "And with Elmore gone…"

Not that she seemed distressed by the circumstances.

"That would be mighty nice," he said. He was curious about where she was taking this. "I'll admit that I get tired of my own company," he said. Then he wanted to push it a little. "Long nights out on the trail make you real aware of being alone."

That awareness wasn't something he didn't really mind, but he wouldn't tell her that. Odds were, the invitation was part and parcel of someone's plan, and that someone figured to be Amy Chancellor. And it started with him bringing Redding the message that would get him out of town.

The best play, the smartest thing to do, would be to travel with the wind at his back and see where it took him.

But keeping his eyes open for traps along the way, of course.

"Right after dark," she said.

It seemed that his acceptance pleased the woman more than was proper. She had something in her head and that suggested she intended the evening to be a matter of more than dinner.

Perhaps Tank Williams being sent out of town the same day Elmore Redding went to the Chancellor ranch was not a coincidence.

When Donna went home, Sam got up and ambled over to the jail.

He walked in and found Douglas sitting at a desk, smoking a cheroot. He had his boots up on the scarred and battered wooden top, his legs crossed at the ankles.

"Well, Sam Colder, I see you couldn't stay away from our dusty paradise," he said, laughing.

"I missed your witty conversation, Douglas," Sam said.

The sheriff waved his arm in a grand gesture, indicating the cells in back. "Your boys are doing fine, as you can see. We even been feeding them, and probably a damn sight better food than they'd been eating out on the trail."

The two pairs of frightened brown eyes staring out at him through the cell bars confirmed what the sheriff was saying.

"Glad to hear it," he said. "The governor will be glad to hear it."

"Well, fuck the governor," Douglas said.

"I take it you didn't vote for him?" Sam asked. "Me, neither, come to think of it. But I didn't vote for the other fella, either."

"Politics!" Douglas spat. "Assholes up in Prescott think they run things."

"In some ways, they do," Sam said.

"You done spying for him yet?"

"For the governor? No. Spying implies there is some secret to uncover," Sam said.

"Or that the governor thinks there is some secret, even if there ain't one."

"Fair point, Sheriff."

"Still got your face set on uncovering some conspiracy here in Rock Canyon?"

"Well, if you know of one and could point me at it, I'd be obliged. Trouble is that, at the moment, I got nothing saying for sure the killings ain't no more than exactly what you told me.." He nodded at the cells. "And after all, you got confessions."

That got Sam a smile. "I most surely do."

"I heard you sent the deputy out scouting for more of them. Or is he after something else?"

Douglas scowled. "I sent him out because the mayor is a nervous Nellie and worries there will be more bandits around. I told Tank to look around because the mayor sleeps better knowing his lawmen are standing a good watch."

"And now he's gone."

Douglas scowled. "Don't that beat all? If I'd known he was gonna be out of town, I wouldn't have bothered. Total waste of time."

"I hope you are right," Sam said. "That it's a waste of time."

Douglas looked surprised. "Do you?"

"I would think it real handy to find your arrests stopped all the killing. I surely would like that. Now, I admit that these fellas don't strike me as the killing type, and I have my doubts about your story."

"Doubts?"

"I've known you to tell a lie or two, Douglas. But I've been wrong about people before. If these men are the killers, well, I'd be happy to admit I got it wrong this time as well."

"Well, don't that beat all?"

"I told you I came here to learn the truth. And you being the one telling the story don't make it any more or less true. And if the truth came from your mouth, it would be a little bitter for me."

"I think that was an insult," Douglas said.

"It was," Sam told him. "And I think I'll go have a drink and wash the bad taste of saying you might be right out of my mouth."

"Now I almost believe you," Douglas said as Sam walked out.

Chapter 13

Donna's Play

The Redding house, a neat, two-story wooden-frame structure, that once might have been painted bright blue, but which had faded to a dull off-white in the blazing desert sun, sat at the end of the street, making it the last building at the west end.

"You like being away from the hubbub of downtown Rock Canyon?" Sam asked as they sat in a spacious, airy parlor. Oil lamps cast shadows that moved as the evening breeze moved in through open windows, flicking the drapes.

Donna blinked at his joke, and he saw that it had misfired completely.

"We expect the town to grow," she said, taking his coat and gun belt and hanging them by the door. "One day soon, this will be right in the center of things."

"Will it?"

Her face reflected a certainty that he found odd.

"When the railroad comes through, this place will boom," she said.

"Through here?"

"Of course."

"I find it curious that you think the railroad will come this far south," he said. "The track they've been laying ain't pointing this way. In fact, I heard tell they are building on a whistlestop they call Maley. That's way the hell up in Sulphur Springs Valley—a fair piece to the north of you. And even a spur... well, it would have to go through some rough country to come here."

"Those matters are all political," she said, as if that made them easy. "If you approach things correctly, approach the right people with the right incentives, well, minds can be changed."

In that observation, she was right... at least until they laid the rail down. That Donna was another damn politician explained a few things in Sam's eyes.

"I suppose they can," he said. "But I'm a practical man and I see the challenges they'd face."

"And we have to help them see the opportunities," she said.

"You are probably right. I don't understand politics at all."

"And yet, here you are, representing the governor of the territory."

"In a rather limited way. To investigate massacres."

"That's a horrid word," she said. "Taints the place."

"But it's accurate. Anyway, my job ain't even remotely political."

Emily came in and Donna Redding put up a hand, signaling that she was putting the conversation on hold as the girl handed them each a drink.

"Dinner is coming along," Emily said.

"Then we should move to the dining room," Donna said.

She led him into the dining room, and they sat. "I never thought you'd be so naïve," she said when Emily disappeared back into the kitchen.

"Is that what I am?"

"Seems like. You say your job ain't political, but you got to see that you being here at all is extremely political. It makes a statement, the governor's statement. He is showing us he intends to be a neutral arbiter of disputes, and therefore make folks think he is a man who can be trusted."

Her grin suggested she didn't trust the man at all.

"Well, in that case, almost anything the man does would be considered political."

She nodded. "Drop the 'almost' and you are right. And the same goes for your Judge March."

"Does it now?"

"That man figures to play a key role in the next phase of the development of the territory."

"What kind of role is that?"

"Winner," she said. "For instance, did you know that the railroad is planning to build themselves a big station in Tucson, and nothing in Prescott?"

"I didn't, but who cares?"

She laughed again.

Emily brought in the dinner and served them.

"That will be all for the evening, Emily," Donna said.

Emily nodded. "I'll be in my room if you need anything," she said.

Donna picked up her fork. "You asked who cares about the railroad in Tucson? I'd guess everyone in the territory, everyone but you, does. The railroad coming to Tucson is gonna bring huge changes. Money, new business, all sorts of progress will come to Tucson. Soon enough, the capital will have to move there."

"Sounds fascinating."

"Well, I've heard that your buddy Judge March is a big property owner down in Tucson and buying more. When they move the capital from Prescott, he'll be rich and influential. You'd do well to keep him as a friend."

"Money and influence ain't the basis I use for choosing my friends, Mrs. Redding."

"Call me Donna, Sam."

"Okay, Donna."

"And I suggest that you expand your ideas about what makes people good friends. A man like Judge March could prove very help-ful to you. And you do better when you got helpful friends."

"That sounds like pretty smart advice, Donna."

"I could be a friend, too," she said. "I ain't as powerful or important as the judge, but hav-ing me for a friend has other advantages."

The flicker in her eyes added significant detail to what those advantages might be.

"I bet it does. And sure, friends are good," he said. "But don't Mayor Elmore frown on his wife having men friends, though?"

"I'm sure he does. But does that mean I can't have them?"

"I don't know. I suppose that is up to you, Donna."

She grinned. "And the men I want to be friends with."

"Naturally."

"They'd have to be man enough that they didn't seriously mind Elmore objecting to that friendship."

"I see."

"You ain't worried about what Elmore thinks, are you?"

"Not particularly," Sam said. "He and I ain't likely to get along well under any circumstances."

Her smile grew. "I don't imagine that troubles you much."

Her obvious meaning got him laughing. She wasn't pretending anything. "I reckon it don't."

They'd finished eating, and she lifted a hand, pointing to the parlor.

"Let's have a drink in the parlor to celebrate our friendship."

He followed her in, his eyes drinking in her fine, lithe body. After all, when something is clearly on offer, it is rude not to at least take a good look.

"To friendship," she said, handing him a glass of whisky.

"To friendship," he said, tasting it and finding it to be good. Not the cheap stuff from the saloon. Mixed with her perfume, which rose from the bare tops of her breasts, it made a heady bouquet.

"You are smiling," she said.

"Straight whisky and warm women are two intoxicating things, and right now I'm getting a strong whiff of both," he said.

"Intoxicating is a flattering word when you use it that way," she said.

"Then it's the right word," he said. "A little whisky and a lot of woman can get a man drunk on pure pleasure."

He drank down the whisky and put his glass on the mantle, then took her by the shoulders and buried his nose between her breasts. As her soft mounds touched his face, her hand went behind his head, and she arched her back.

Sam put a hand on her ass and held her to him while his other hand went to her back to fumble with the laces of her dress. His fingers quickly unhooked the laces, and he lifted his face, watching hers as he pulled the dress down her shoulders, exposing her breast.

Leaning forward, he sucked a nipple into his mouth and sucked it. She let out a little gasp and the nub hardened in his mouth, even as his hands continued working her dress down her body.

"You are taking advantage of our new friendship," she said.

"Yes, I am. But friends do give friends what they want," he said, staring deep into her eyes. "And, I'm pretty sure that you know exactly where to find what you want."

She did. And she began undoing his pants.

The lady was naked under the dress and when the dress was on the floor and his pants at his knees with his cock in her hand, he kissed her, forcing his tongue in her mouth. Her breath was ragged as they broke the kiss and he put his hand on her cunt, letting his fingers enter her. She was wet.

"I'm going to fuck you," he said.

Giving him a wide-eyed smile, she looked into his eyes. "Yes, fuck the mayor's wife."

He turned her to face the mantle, bending her over. She put out her hands, bracing herself as he spread her legs apart. He held his cock and stepped close, bringing his swollen prick to her pussy. She wiggled her hips enticingly as he penetrated her, then she bent over more, and he gripped her hips and drove deep and a soft moan reached his ears.

"So good," she said as he took her, fucking her steadily.

He'd enjoy what the woman offered tonight. The next day, he wanted to ride out again and see the Walker homestead. It seemed to play a key role here. The Mexican woman had seen the five men who arrested the Mexicans raiding the homestead. Douglas claimed to have found tracks leading to a camp.

Sam had to admit to being biased about which story he believed. It was important to find some hard evidence.

But for now, Donna's body had his attention. Her wet and warm cunt caressed his cock, getting him ready to explode.

And when he came, he was already thinking about fucking her again.

Chapter 14

Intensifying the Offense

A day later, Mark Douglas found himself as close to heaven as a man could get in this shithole town and that was having his hard prick thrusting inside Donna Redding's cunt. The woman could be a right bitch at times, and controlling, too, but spread her legs wide, and he was willing to admit she was a great fuck.

Lying between her soft thighs, with her wrapping those legs around him as he drove his hard cock into her, was something special. Partly it was that the mayor's wife squealed and writhed, and generally didn't mind letting a man know how much she enjoyed having a hard cock stuffed in her tight cunt the way some women did.

Part of his pleasure came from the fact that he was cuckolding the idiot mayor. That tickled him. And now, as he pounded into Donna, coming in the mayor's wife, he was finding being a sheriff pretty good.

The only thing bothering him was the suspicion that Sam Colder was getting some of this pussy, too. He'd stayed a long time at her house when he went over for dinner.

But he'd be damned if he'd ask Donna. She'd like that. She'd like the idea that he cared who she was fucking. And maybe it was that Amy's idea for her to fuck Colder. That might give them some control over Colder. It wasn't any different than her fucking him. He knew she did it to get what she wanted. That was what women did.

Although he liked the way that worked for him right then, well enough.

"I need you to get things going with them homesteaders again," she said.

"It's a little difficult with the governor's man here," he said. She should see that.

"What about your men? Why didn't they take care of him?"

He shook his head. "It's just me and Tank. I can't find those sonsabitches. I ain't seen or heard from them since I sent them out to ambush Colder."

"He kill them?"

"He ain't said shit. When he got here, you'd think he had the most boring trip ever, so I don't know. I sent Tank out to find them and tell them he was heading out to the ranches. I thought maybe they'd gotten drunk or something, but he said they weren't at the camp we agreed on."

"Well, then we need to get more men."

"In this remote place, getting men that won't cut our throats in our sleep is tough."

"Look here, Mark, we need to get the homesteaders running for the hills. Now, having them Mexicans in jail bought us some time, but it's also got people buzzing with worry. You stage a couple more attacks and they'll all run for the hills."

"But we are supposed to have captured the bandits. We got them ready to confess. They don't tell the judge the story we gave them, we will kill their families."

"We can use them in a different way," Donna said. "Amy came up with a good idea."

"Amy did?"

"If these cutthroats happened to escape from jail, well, there is no telling what mischief they'd get up to," she said.

"Escaped? That ain't about to happen. I ain't a proper sheriff, but I can keep a couple of Mexicans in jail."

"I know you can," she said. "That's why they are gonna need your help in breaking out."

"My help?"

She nodded. "Here's how it works. The moon is slim now and the nights are dark. While there ain't no light to see by proper, you need to take those Mexicans out in the desert somewhere,"

"Why?"

"Get them far enough away from town that no one will hear gunshots, and you shoot them dead. Then bury them deep. No shallow grave. Deep enough so no one stumbles over the bodies for a long time."

"Why kill them? They don't know shit. We can just send them running for the border. They are so fucking scared they won't hang around here for a minute."

"Think about it," she said, softly. "We have told everyone that Mexican bandits are killing people. If you let them go, what happens if some homesteaders catch them? Of what if they run to Sam Colder? We can't risk anyone knowing you let them go on purpose."

He got her point. "So, if I shoot them..."

"That shuts them up," she said. "There is no way they can tell anyone anything. And Colder can't go telling the governor that the good folks of Rock Canyon took the law into our own hands."

"Colder won't believe they broke out."

"That's why you need to shoot Tank."

"Shoot my deputy?"

"You get horses ready, then, while he is taking care of the prisoners, you go in and shoot him and take the prisoners out in the desert, like I said. The story is that the rest of the banditos showed up, killed Tank, and broke their amigos out."

Douglas could see that. The story hung together.

"Why not just wound Tank?"

"No. You got to shoot him dead."

"Kill Tank? Why?"

"I told you that anyone you hire is expendable."

"Yeah, you said that."

"Well, him being dead does two things. First, it makes it clear just how vicious these bandits are, shooting a man in cold blood like that. Reminds them that these are the people who slaughtered homesteaders."

"Yeah, makes sense."

"Besides, sooner or later he's gotta go. Thank knows too much, and he ain't bright enough to know what to keep secret. He could spill the beans on us."

"He's a good boy."

"And a big risk. Mark, we got us to the point where you don't need him anymore. This way, his death is part of the story. The story that the rest of the bandits came into town in the night, shot Tank and rescued their amigos is one even Colder will buy."

Mark smiled. "And where was I? In your bed?"

She laughed. "Maybe fucking Emily, or just sleeping. But when you walk in and find Tank dead, you head out to track the bastards down and bring them to justice."

"A pointless ride."

"No, because after you kill the Mexicans, I want you to attack another homestead."

"So soon?"

"Remember, the story is that the goddamn Mexicans got themselves in a killing mood during the escape. Once they are free, they let off steam by attacking another homestead on their way back down to Mexico or wherever."

"I kill more homesteaders?"

"Right. Then when you go back out to hunt down Tank's killers, you discover the latest massacre and come back to report it."

Mark lay back on the bed, picturing how that would play out. Unless Colder didn't see him taking the prisoners out of town, it was pretty good.

"What about Colder?"

"What about him?"

"He don't trust me. He's keeping an eye out."

She laughed. "That's why you do it in the dark," she said. "He can't see shit with no moon."

There were about a dozen things wrong with her take on that, but Mark Douglas was starting to put together his own ideas about what to do next, and he didn't want to chew them over with Donna. She wouldn't understand.

"Seems like that plan you and Amy put together has me doing a lot of hard work here," he said. "And taking the risk. All of it, actually."

"That's why we hired you," she said.

He shook his head. "No, Chancellor hired me to carry out a simple plan. As sheriff, he told me I was to capture some bandits and make sure they confessed to the killings. Make sure they'd be willing to tell a judge they did it. Later on, you and your sister added some new bits."

"Did we?" she asked, grinning.

"You made it pretty damn clear, Donna. When the land is all government land again, once them homesteaders are dead or left without living up to their five-year promise, well, then you want me to arrange a couple of accidents so you and your sister can run the whole place. You expect me to arrange accidents for both Chancellor and the mayor."

She reached for his cock and wrapped her fingers around it. "And ain't I rewarding you for your trouble?"

He swallowed. She knew he wanted her again.

Sneaking around for pussy, keeping people from knowing you were fucking a woman, was a pain because even when you did it well, it never gave you enough time to get all you wanted.

"The fucking is fine, but if you want your husbands out of the way... hell, I'm taking a risk."

"So, think of this as two different deals, different games going on, Mark. Amy got her husband to hire you for the bandits. That's right.

The pleasure I've been giving you ain't for anything, except for pleasure itself. But you are getting more now than you was promised. And when the homesteaders is gone, after things calm down, we can talk about payment to do them other little favors. I'm sure I can keep you happy with the deal."

"After things calm down?" he asked.

"It can't happen real soon. Them both dying right after? No. And we can't have both of them having accidents too close together, or it might be suspicious."

"They can have the accidents anytime," he said.

"That wouldn't look right," she said.

"Look right to who? We kill them and just don't tell no one. None of the folks in town are going to ask questions, and no one else will even know they are dead."

"What's the rush?" Donna asked.

"Because, once Elmore is out of the way, we won't have to find something for him to do before we can spend a day in bed screwing. I hate the playacting."

"Not having to sneak around would make it better," she said. "We could live together, even."

He wrinkled his nose, imagining it. "You won't expect me to marry you, will you?"

Her fingers, wrapped firmly around his dick, had it hard again.

"I wouldn't marry you on a bet, Mark."

"I got to think about the price for arranging those accidents," he said.

"Oh, come on, you know Amy and I will make it worth your while. We can arrange something," she said. "Maybe we should make you mayor. How would you like that?"

It sounded good for a moment.

"I think I like being sheriff better," he said. It surprised him to hear those words out of his own mouth, but they were true. He was enjoying the power and prestige. Better yet, he saw a different, brighter future for himself than Donna saw. Working for these bitches after he killed their husbands didn't make sense.

No, being sheriff was better. When he got tired of their uppity nonsense, of living in Rock Canyon, there wouldn't be anyone to keep him from emptying the cash from this town and taking it with him.

And he knew there was cash around. These people, the Reddings and Chancellors, and the Evert family too, used the general store as sort of a bank. It had a nice safe, and they kept the money for cattle purchases and sales there, as well as money for supply runs.

It wasn't a fortune, but it would be more than Mark Douglas had ever seen in one place, and he intended to leave with it.

He ran a hand over Donna's breast and decided he'd bide his time. He was in no rush to move on.

When the job was done, after that sono-fabitch Colder was dead, he could hang around here for a while in peace. Taking care of the husbands, helping Donna and her sister Amy lose their old men wouldn't be a big deal. Chancellor was old and Redding an idiot with no gun sense.

Staying around for a time, he could fuck Donna every which way and live like a king for a bit. Maybe he'd treat Amy to a taste of what a real man offered a woman, too.

Even if both women were happy to spread their legs for him, Rock Canyon was a shit hole and life here would grow old soon enough. Besides, these conniving women probably had some big plan that probably wouldn't include him.

So, eventually, he'd leave this shitty little place, but he'd leave as a rich man.

While Donna wouldn't mind him moving on at all, he enjoyed imagining the shocked look, the horror on Donna's face when she found out he'd taken the money with him. The conniving bitch would be furious when she learned that all the money she'd thought was going to be hers was gone.

"I'm sure we can work out a deal," he told her.

He trailed his fingers over her ass, letting them slip into the crack and press meaningfully into her anus. The way her eyes opened wide made him smile. "We can be snug partners, Donna."

"Mark—"

"You and me are going to get real tight," he told her. "Well, I'll be inside that tight little hole."

Her expression told him she'd give him what he wanted. And he didn't count on getting anything later that she wouldn't give him now.

Chapter 15

Escape Plans

Tank looked tired when he rode into town. Searching for men in the desert does that.

"Come in my room and take a seat," Douglas told him. "I got a bottle."

Tank nodded. He looked unhappy.

"Any luck?" Mark asked.

Tank shook his head. "Couldn't find a trace of them," he said. "I went to the ravine where they was supposed to ambush Colder and found some dried blood. There could be bodies out there, I didn't look up in the rocks."

"The blood weren't Colder's," Douglas said. "The fucking cowards must have run off."

"Or he killed them," Tank said. "If they tried to jump Colder like you were paying them to do, and it went south, he might have shot them."

"All three?" Mark wasn't ready to accept that.

Tank only shrugged. "I didn't trust them boys."

"We couldn't find better men on short no-tice," Mark said. "Don't matter now."

He poured them both drinks and Tank drank gratefully. Douglas didn't have many friends, and he'd miss Tank.

"What now?"

"We got a little more work to do, and seeing as we can't get good help, it seems we got to do it ourselves."

"You got a new plan?" Tank asked. He finished his drink and refilled his glass.

Mark nodded. Sitting on his bed, he took out his Colt. He unloaded it and began cleaning it while he explained the plan to Tank.

The plan he explained wasn't exactly Donna's plan, although his was similar. It was still based on her idea of pretending the Mexicans escaped. Killing the Mexicans was the part of the plan he liked best. It got them out of his hair. But he made changes.

Donna didn't believe that Colder was already suspicious of him, of the entire idea. And she didn't understand how that affected her plan. There was no way a suspicious Colder would fall for the idea that amigos of the two in jail showed up out of nowhere, killed Tank, and then rode off, stopping off on their way out of town to kill more homesteaders.

Sure, it was a story that Chancellor would like, and everyone else, maybe even that damn judge in Prescott would buy into, but Colder knew his Mexicans almost as good as he knew his Indians. If the bandits rode into town to rescue their pals, they'd come in shooting, making a lot of noise. They'd kill a bunch of people. And when Colder looked and didn't find a bunch of tracks leading into town, he'd spot the lie right off.

So Sam Colder had to die.

And there was one of the big problems with her plan—it left Mark Douglas to kill Sam Colder all by himself. He didn't much like the odds of that. Especially if Colder had killed the three men he'd sent to ambush him.

It pissed him off that the morons he had hired, the ones he sent to ambush him, hadn't done their job. The ambush should have worked, and killing him out there would have made things simple. The man never arrives and there is no problem. If anyone inquires about him, no one ever saw him. So who knew what happened to him?

Now, he would have to take care of it himself.

Mark Douglas wasn't afraid of Colder, not for an instant. He'd killed meaner, faster men. Still, the man had a reputation for being as dangerous as a snake. And Douglas had no intention of facing him down. No, he'd be careful, find a way to catch him with his guard down.

He had some ideas, but they would have to come after he took care of the Mexicans.

Having Colder watching the way he did, hanging around, taking in everything, gave him the creeps.

In the best of all worlds, Mark Douglas would simply do what needed to be done himself. But Chancellor was paying him to make things look a certain way, and his wife's plan made some sense. The problem with it was that he couldn't kill Tank in the jail. He needed his deputy's help to execute a better plan, one that required two people to carry out. Without Tank, that would require him to be in two places at once.

But his plan had a cost. He had to get Tank to understand his role clearly. Have it exactly right. He had to make sure the man had it straight in that thick skull of his.

Now he took his time explaining it, cleaning his Colt as he talked, pausing to take measured sips of his whisky, as he broke the plan down into simple steps and then explained each one. Speaking slowly and carefully, glancing at the man's face, he made sure the man got it, and got it right.

Then, patiently, he made the deputy repeat every step back to him, saying it out loud. For Tankheart Williams had a very bad habit of saying, "sure, I got it," when he didn't have a fucking clue what you had told him. He liked to be positive, Tank did. Didn't want to disappoint anyone, Tank didn't. Especially someone like Mark Douglas.

Mark had learned those hard lessons about Tank through experience.

At first, he'd thought Tank was unreliable, but he came to see that he was just thick and had trouble figuring things out. But like anyone, he didn't like admitting he was in a fog to himself or anyone else.

He didn't want to kill Tank. The guy was good to have around, and reliable when he knew what to do. But Donna was right about him and the danger he represented. He didn't have the sense to work out what not to tell people. And that could cause trouble down the line.

But having the law after him wasn't that big a deal. Nothing new.

More important, more near and dear to Mark's heart, was the problem of the money. If Tank was around when he took all the money he could find and left, the big guy might expect a share of it.

No way was that gonna happen. Better to nip those things in the bud.

For once, that inability to understand things, to see what was in front of his face, would be an asset. For Mark. Tank would never think Mark would double-cross him, never see it coming. And that's what he intended to do.

If things went right, and they killed the Mexicans and Colder, he'd have a free hand. But Tank would be useful, so he wouldn't kill Tank the way Donna wanted.

No, he'd find some way to get Chancellor and the Mayor to ride out somewhere, even if just to the Chancellor's ranch. Then he and Tank would follow and kill them. When they were dead, he'd put a bullet in Tank. He'd come back to town and say he and Tank were out looking for the bandits, but he didn't find them. Sooner or later, someone would find the bodies and they'd decide the bandits killed them.

That would be a damn sight better than trying to arrange some fucking accident for them.

Faster, more certain.

Chapter 16
Sorting Things Out

Sam sat in a chair he'd rocked back against the saloon wall. His feet, legs crossed, pressed against one of the uprights and he smoked a cigarette, taking leisurely puffs as he thought things through. He idly pictured the chain of events.

But one of those lazy thoughts had nothing to do with his investigation at all... or it had to do with all his investigations. For it occurred to him that he had probably spent more of his life sitting in saloons waiting for shit to happen than doing just about anything else, or being anywhere else.

That wasn't a regret or some idea that he was wasting time... it wasn't anything but one of those odd: "Here I am sitting in a saloon again, waiting," thoughts.

Weird thoughts popped up and surprised him when he waited.

Another thought appeared in that strange space in his head that was about Claire Reed. She could have gotten his letter by now. She could have answered. He hoped she agreed to come to Prescott. That would make Thelma happy, and the more he thought about it, the more he thought it would be good to see Claire again. She was a hell of a woman. He was glad she was being a success. She worked for it. Took the risks.

And then those thoughts faded, dropping him back in the Rock Canyon saloon, sipping the really bad whisky the saloon sold, and thinking about some of the really dreadful people that lived in and around the town.

Saloons were not the nicest places, certainly not the best places to sit, but doing the kind of thing he did, hunting people, hunting information, took him to them often. Every town had a saloon, and they were often the hub, the one place you could count on seeing everyone in town, except maybe the church people, and Rock Canyon had a dire shortage of the meek who expected to inherit the earth.

No, in a desert scrub town like this, most people figured that the ones in line to inherit anything were the ones bold and sometimes mean enough to hold onto them.

With luck, his visit to Chancellor and letting folks know that he wasn't about to take things at face value had stirred things up. They wanted things settled, and he was in the way. As Jubal had said, this was the time of year the ranchers wanted their cattle out grazing, and that would limit their patience with him investigating. Soon, if they were going to get the homesteaders out, they'd need to make another move.

If Chancellor had made getting the homesteaders out a condition of Mark Douglas' employment, the way it seemed, then the sheriff would be feeling some pressure.

That was all fine, and waiting wasn't a problem. But 'wait and see' included two actions and Sam couldn't watch Tank Williams and Mark Douglas at the same time. Again, trusting his gut, they'd be the ones who would try and move things along.

While Mark Douglas was a hands-on person in many ways, when it came to doing all the sneaky shit, Sam had no doubt that he wouldn't mind assigning chores to his deputy. He'd know Sam had eyes on him.

It was a situation, all right. Sam had to guess, and he didn't much like guessing when lives were at stake, and most of the ways he saw this working out, the sheriff or the deputy would be setting their faces to kill someone.

So, when it came time to flip a coin, he spent the coin on a drink instead and decided that it made more sense to watch the jail and not either of them.

After a couple of drinks, he'd convinced himself that Douglas was overly concerned about Sam's interest in giving the Mexicans a fair shake. If the things he'd been told were even close to the truth, Chancellor wouldn't want to risk putting the alleged bandits in front of a judge to talk under oath. No matter what leverage they were using, and Sam was pretty sure he had that figured, a trial would risk having the real story come out.

So, no one wanted a trial.

The only way to prevent that was to eliminate the need for one. And that meant getting rid of the prisoners somehow. Or getting rid of him. Or both.

That third option seemed the most likely. With him gone, there wouldn't be any report to the governor, and sending someone to replace him gave them more than enough time. Hell, if Sam disappeared and someone found his body out in the desert, the sheriff could say he stumbled across the bandits and got blown away. If the Mexicans were gone, escaped somehow, and then the raids started up again, well, then they could blame the Mexicans for all of it.

And who would be left to say otherwise?

That got him feeling a totally different kind of loneliness than the kind he'd talked to Donna Redding about. The kind he'd mentioned to her was just the absence of companionship, something fairly easily remedied. A quick fuck with a warm and willing woman did a lot to ease that pain.

This loneliness was a lot more threatening because it was an awareness that you had no one to cover your back.

And out here, you needed to feel you had your back covered or face the fact that you were vulnerable. And at least two men, two armed men, didn't want him to continue his investigation.

Chapter 17
Jailbreak

A shot fired inside a building during the night can come across as a muffled crack, a vague pop. Yet, to those who have been in gunfights, around gunfire, it's a distinctive sound, as unique as the crack of a bullwhip, and quite different.

With the shot triggering an alert in his brain, Sam came awake at the sound, sitting upright, and reaching for his carbine, which he had leaned against the wall be the door. Chambering a round, he stepped out of the room and walked past the saloon to the main street.

No one else ventured out onto the street. In towns like this, curiosity could be fatal.

The commotion, as expected, came from the jail, and the subsequent drama that played out was rather predictable. As Sam watched from the shadows, four men came out of the jail and scrambled up onto waiting horses. From his size, one of them had to be Tank.

"So, the sheriff arranges the jailbreak," Sam muttered. "Efficient."

Sam stepped back into the shadows to the spot behind his room where Rocky waited, saddled, eager to go.

He mounted and followed the men out of town at a steady pace, heading north, out into the dry, flat expanse of nothing that filled miles of space in that direction.

Even in the dark, the trail was easy to follow. They made no attempt to hide their sign and didn't ride at the blistering pace of men worried a posse might be in pursuit.

Sam wondered who had designed this plan for Douglas. While he was a bushwhacker and setting traps was second nature to him, the drama in town wasn't his style. It was too subtle and clever. Subtle, clever, and irresistible. If Sam followed them, they would spring a trap and kill him. If he didn't follow, they would kill the prisoners and put out the story that the men escaped and dare Sam to prove otherwise.

Either way, they eliminated the chance of a trail, the opportunity for the truth to come out.

Riding slowly, not wanting to accidentally catch up with them, the back of Sam's neck felt the tickling caress of a cold wind creeping down the hills from the mountains. If he'd been hunting wolves he might have worried it would change direction and carry his scent ahead of him, warning his prey. But men, except for a few Indians and mountain men he'd met, didn't notice such things as a warm animal smell drifting toward them.

A mark of just how good the plan was lay in the fact that him knowing the basics of their plan, their intentions being obvious, didn't matter. The Mexicans served as bait, with Sam's desire for justice forcing his hand. They'd made it clear that they intended to kill them and trusted that Sam would feel obligated to show up and try to stop them.

Leaving town in the dark gave Mark Douglas and his deputy a tremendous advantage. Certainly, they'd have picked out a place where, by arriving first, they'd hand themselves the high ground and the best cover. Sam, or anyone following them, would have to approach over open ground.

All he could do was stay behind and wait to see how it unfolded. Keeping his promise to the wives of those men, that he'd do his best to protect them, meant taking the risk. Outgunned, he had few options but to play the hand he was being dealt.

As he rode, he became aware of stealthy movements shadowing him off to the side, moving at their pace. When Rocky twitched, snorting and jerking at the reins, that told him all he needed to know. Wolves. Probably Mexican grays. They were the only creature he'd come across that spooked Rocky. Ever.

It had the horse on edge, but now he settled and Sam went back to second-guessing himself.

As much as he disliked letting Douglas' plan play out, he had few choices. One man couldn't easily arrest the two lawmen as the homesteader killers, especially not when they had the support of the mayor and Chancellor. The rancher could claim he was the lawbreaker. Probably send in ranch hands to get their sheriff out. Then Sam would have his hands full with a legal and physical battle and he couldn't predict how those would come out. If he lost, the Mexicans would be in danger and he'd be no closer to finishing his job.

That led him to consider the one other possibility—gunning the two lawmen down. Again, he didn't have legal proof they were the killers. He had witnesses who would say that the sheriff had lied about how they captured the Mexicans, and the homesteaders had their suspicions, but he couldn't prove that the two men were anything more than lazy and greedy lawmen.

He couldn't justify shooting them in cold blood, which left him trying to goad them into drawing on him. Even if he managed that, that made it two to one. And a gunfight in town risked other innocent lives.

There weren't a lot of people in Rock Canyon, but none of the people working there deserved to be shot just because they were there.

So, it came down to this—watching them carry out their plan and hoping he could find a moment, and a place, to turn the tables.

When a large rock formation loomed off to his right, up a slight slope, Sam reined Rocky in and looked at it.

The desert was still, telling him nothing, but this formation was exactly the kind of spot he would choose for an ambush—a few large boulders sat in a rough circle with a small opening leading into a clear area.

A fire flickered in the clearing in the center and he was sure the prisoners would be there. They were pretending to set up camp for the night.

The Mexicans would be the bait to lure him in where they had a clear shot, while the rocks provided the shooters with an excellent view and plenty of cover. They could easily pick all three of them off.

Urging Rocky forward, then turning to circle around behind the formation, Sam dismounted.

He'd worn his moccasins again, and now he was more than glad. They made it easier to climb. Not that the rocks were big or high, but quiet was his only advantage, and boots that were perfect for riding were impossible to climb in quietly.

The position he found himself in wasn't as dire as he'd expected. Douglas and Williams might be confident he was coming, but they couldn't know exactly when he'd get there.

With luck, he'd approached slowly and quietly enough that they wouldn't know he was there already.

Not yet.

Scanning the tops of the rocks, he looked for the best places for a man to position to fire down. With two men, the clever thing would be to have the other watching the open land in case he saw the formation and decided to circle, as Sam had done.

A trap within a trap.

He heard a howl off to his right. The damn wolves were closing in. Above him, he saw a shadowy movement tucked up against one of the rocks.

Marking that spot, Sam circled around, looking for the second shooter.

Hoofbeats rose up, echoing on the rocks. He glanced out and saw a rider leaving, heading off, but not going back toward town.

The rest of their plan came to him then, and he cursed himself. He'd been an idiot. The ambush was just one piece of the plan, a diversion. Now, with their trap set, one of them had headed out for the Holloway homestead.

With the Mexicans on the loose, he could kill the homesteaders and blame it on the escapees.

Slick and ugly.

Backing quietly, he found the spot where he'd seen the shooter. With his elbow resting on a rock, still warm from the day's sunlight, he took careful aim. It wasn't a long shot, just tricky. He waited until he saw a man-shaped movement. He didn't have a clear shot. Staring into the dark mass, he couldn't rightly tell where the rock ended, and the man started.

Again, a wolf howled, and this time a growl followed it. The shrill whinny of a horse shot through him.

Rocky!

The shadow on the boulders moved, and Sam saw the bright muzzle flash of his rifle firing and heard the crack of the shot.

Sam let out a breath and squeezed the trigger. The rifle recoiled into his shoulder. His shot rang out and he smelled the acrid stink of gunpowder. There was a cry of pain and the clatter of rock sliding down the slope. He levered the carbine, aimed, and fired into the shadowy blob again.

Another clatter reached his ears, then the dull thud that had to be a body striking the rocks below. And then it was quiet.

Sam made his way down and found Tank's crumpled body. Both shots had hit him.

Climbing down to the clearing in the center, he found the two Mexicans sitting back-to-back, tied together. A few feet away, three horses stood hobbled.

Sam pulled a knife and cut their bonds, telling them in his border Spanish to take their horses and ride home.

"Stay out of sight for a couple of days," he said. "Then, if you hear the sheriff is dead, you and your families are safe. If he ain't dead, you best head down south because it means he killed me."

One, named Hector, he remembered, grabbed Sam and hugged him. "*Vaya con dios*," he said.

The other grabbed the horses, and they got up and rode off.

Sam went to where he'd left Rocky with his heart pounding. As he stepped toward the spot, fierce growls greeted him. Two wolves, fangs bared, stared at him. They stood over Rocky's dead body and Sam had disturbed their feast.

Sam fired twice. One wolf fell over and the other let out a wail and ducked into the brush.

Rocky was dead. Tank's bullet, fired in the direction of what he thought was an incoming rider, had hit the horse in the head.

"Damn!" he said.

It tore him up to walk away from his friend's body, but the Holloways were in danger. If he moved fast, he might keep them alive.

He swallowed the heartache and rage welling up and went back to get Tank's horse.

"We need to go fast, boy," he said as he swung into the saddle. "That bastard Douglas has murder in mind, and I promised to stop him."

Chapter 18

Nighttime Intruder

Jubal Holloway was certain something was up.

Often, the darkest nights made him edgy. Not being able to see anything but shadows on the ground while a million stars shone down brightly could be unsettling. It made the animal noises more threatening and the world more mysterious.

It was at times like that, on nights like this, that he sometimes questioned their decision to homestead.

Usually, that feeling didn't last. Like the droughts and the flash floods, soon enough, that dread went away on its own. There wasn't much you could do about drought or flood, or dread, for that matter, except get on with things. That's how you survived.

One eerie thing about dark nights, the really black ones, was how you felt like you were being watched.

Crazy.

He cursed himself for reacting like a boy. He was a man now, with a wife.

He was a careful man who kept a carbine close at hand. Not that he expected trouble, but just because there wasn't some evil watching him, it didn't mean that a wolf, or something worse, wasn't prowling around.

Carrying the rifle was being ready, not being scared.

Even with the rifle at hand, Jubal couldn't sleep and sat in a chair watching Charity, who lay in the bed, breathing deeply. Just looking at her made him feel good. Until he heard the hoofbeats.

The pounding of a shod horse on the hard-packed dirt came toward them. A lone rider in the middle of the night, the dark night. Almost no one came out this way. And no one came bringing good news.

Jubal sat, trying to decide if he even wanted to know who the rider was. The knot in his stomach knew that he couldn't ignore the rider.

A smart man sitting in a dark house with a wife he wanted to protect had a responsibility. Jubal wasn't a fighter. He'd never hurt another man in his life, other than breaking Billy Russell's nose in grade school. If he was smart, the thing to do was to crack a shutter just enough to point the barrel of the rifle out, wait until he saw movement that looked like a man, and shoot—several times.

Yet, there was the possibility that the rider might be someone in trouble, a man looking for help, and the thought nagged at him.

And Jubal Holloway tried to be a fair man. But finding out meant opening the door. Opening the door meant putting Charity at risk.

The rider pulled up outside the door. "Holloway," the man shouted. "Holloway, there's been a jailbreak."

Charity stirred and Jubal went to the window, cracking it slightly, but, instead of poking the barrel of his rifle through, he put an eye there. Having heard the voice, he recognized the shadowy figure of Sheriff Douglas.

The man's presence gave him no comfort at all.

"What do you want from me?" he asked.

"Ah," Douglas said. "You are awake."

"I am. But I'm not leaving my home to chase down some abused Mexicans you went and let escape."

"Think about it, man. You got yourself a pretty wife in there," the sheriff said. "These bandits might kill her, or even do worse. They might rape her and kill her."

Sweat streamed down Jubal's face. His dislike for the man had been instinctive, but these claims were bogus.

"And if I go off with you, she would be here alone."

The sheriff pushed on the door but Jubal knew it was thick and held in place by a thick bar.

"Not if we catch them," Douglas said. "Open the door and we can talk."

Now he was certain that Sheriff Douglas was part of this scheme. "Go away. You work for Chancellor. And I think you are the bandit," Jubal said.

"Don't make this harder than it is already," Douglas said.

"What do you mean?"

"I work for the mayor," he said calmly. "But yes, Chancellor pays me and he wants you and your kind gone. That's why I'm here. It's your turn to leave."

"I have a gun," Jubal said.

"But will you use it?" Sheriff Douglas asked.

"Of course, I will."

"Lots of men think that until they see another man in the sights and it is time to pull the trigger. That's when they often freeze and all is lost because, at heart, they are cowards. Boot Hill is full of men like that."

Jubal couldn't make out his hands, but he knew, without looking, that his knuckles were white. He had no idea if he could shoot a man, but now...

"I'm not a coward," Jubal said.

"Tank will be along shortly. Once he takes care of some other business."

Jubal swallowed. The threat was probably true.

"But I don't want to wait for him." Douglas laughed. "Hell, dumb as he is, he might even forget to come. But here is your choice. You can wake your wife, pack your things and leave right now. I'll wave goodbye to you. But if I have to wait for Tank to get here, then we are going to set fire to your house. When it gets nice and hot, when you can't breathe no more from all the smoke and you come running out, I'll gun you down."

His heart pounded. There was no doubt that Douglas would do exactly that.

"That's plain murder," he said.

Douglas snorted. "That's right. Exactly what it is. Although if we have to go to that trouble, we probably won't gun down the wife. She's right pretty as I recall. Me and Tank can have some fun for a time, then sell her to a whore-house in Sonora for a good price."

Jubal felt his rage building, along with a feeling of helplessness, exactly what Douglas wanted.

"You are an animal," he said.

Douglas chuckled. "Been called worse. Done worse, for that matter. But it's your choice."

A choice that was no choice. If they packed and left, Douglas would do exactly the same thing. After what had happened to the other homesteaders, he wouldn't allow them to leave, to carry their story to another town, or to risk it reaching the governor.

Jubal wasn't a fighter, but he wasn't a coward or an idiot. Men like Douglas had to be stopped, whatever the cost.

The shape that was Douglas got down off his horse. "I bet there is an oil lamp in the barn," he said. "That'll do just fine. As dry as things are, if I toss a little of your hay on the roof, light the lamp and throw it up there, that should get things, and you, cooking nicely."

For a time, he was quiet. The silence collapsed on them. Then he heard a long breath.

"Well, if you want it this way, that's fine."

He heard the crunch of boots on the dirt, heading toward the barn. Then all was quiet.

Jubal worked the breech and put a round in the chamber of his rifle. Then he sat it on the window ledge.

He heard a movement and saw Charity sitting up, her arms clutched across her breasts. She'd been listening and her face glowed pale.

Jubal put a finger to his lips, not sure if she could see it. "Shh," he said. "Don't move."

All too soon, the footsteps returned, coming closer, accompanied by the clank and squeak of the metal handle of the lantern.

"It pains me to have to do this," Douglas said. "Mostly because then I'll have to fuck your woman on the hard dirt. It would be much more spreading those thighs apart right in your bed. Wouldn't that be better, Mrs. Holloway?"

Charity was rigid with fear.

Jubal felt her fear, and it made him ashamed. He had the job of protecting her.

The clanking was in front of him. He could make out the figure of a man, and that was as clean a shot as he was going to get. He aimed and squeezed off a shot.

"Goddam!" Douglas howled.

Jubal worked the spent cartridge out of the breech and fumbled for a new one.

A flash of light blinded him, a roar deafened him, and a 44-caliber bullet struck him, slamming him back against the wall.

"Jubal!" Charity screamed.

His arm went numb, and the cartridge fell out of his hand and rolled across the floor.

"Well, then I will burn you out, you dumb fucker. And I hope you decide not to run out. I'll stand here waiting for both of you. I'm in a rush, so I'll settle for hearing your screams as you burn. That will suit me fine."

"That ain't gonna happen," another voice said.

"Colder!" Douglas said.

Jubal crawled to the window and saw the men facing each other. Colder held a rifle on the sheriff.

"Put the lantern down, Mark," Colder said.

"Why? You ain't gonna shoot a man in cold blood. You're a fucking lawman."

"You willing to bet your life on that?" Sam asked. "I am a bounty hunter, after all."

"And one who is known for being fair. You won't shoot a man who don't have a gun in his hand."

"Wrong," Sam said. And he fired.

In the light of the blast, Jubal saw the shot hit Douglas squarely, knocking him down. Sam worked the lever on the rifle, stepped closer to the sheriff, pointed it at his head, and calmly fired again.

"You killed him," Jubal said. Amazement, disbelief, and relief rushed through him.

"Thank God!" Charity said.

Then she was crying, and Jubal went to her, hugging her with his good arm.

"You hurt bad?" Sam called through the door.

"He ain't so bad," Charity said. "I can take care of him fine."

Jubal looked at her and saw that she was already pulling herself together as frontier women did.

"It's in the shoulder," Jubal said.

"Did the bullet go through, or is it stuck in there?" Sam asked. "If you gotta dig it out, you might need some help."

Jubal laughed. "I don't even know," he said, but Charity was already turning him, checking his back. "Looks like I got two holes to patch in this boy. But he ain't bleeding as bad as a body might expect."

"Get a fire going and cauterize it, then pour alcohol on it so it don't go green."

"I know that much, sir," she said.

"Sorry to be a fussbudget, Missus Holloway. I guess I'll just get this dead outlaw off your porch. I'll stick him on his horse and take his sorry ass back to town."

"Thank you," Charity called out.

"It was a real pleasure, Ma'am," Sam said. "A real pleasure. I think you are safe now, but you keep that thick door well barred, and that wound clean."

"I've got Jubal's gun handy," she said. "We'll be fine now."

Then she grabbed scissors and cut away Jubal's shirt and took a closer look at his wound. "

Jubal looked at her. "You know, that man, Colder, he shot the sheriff when he didn't even have a gun in his hand," Jubal said. "Then when he hit the ground, he shot him again."

"Good for him," Charity said. "Damn good thing. And good for you for taking the first shot. Now shut your trap while I get the fire started. If you can, fetch that bottle of whisky we keep under the bed. We are going to need it."

Watching his wife, suddenly calm, suddenly in complete control, the pain from the bullet wasn't nearly so bad. In fact, it didn't hardly hurt at all.

Chapter 19

The Details are Devils

The night was warm, and the desert wind wouldn't pick up until dawn. He didn't worry about making time. There was no rush now.

Despite what he told the Holloways, Sam wasn't riding to town. Swinging into the saddle it dawned on him what had to happen next.

Leading Douglas' horse, he picked his way across the scrubland back to where he'd left Tank. The deputy's body was right where he'd left it, and he dumped the sheriff's body right next to it. Large chunks of Tank's body had been eaten away while Sam was hunting Douglas, probably by the wolves, but that didn't matter. And that's what wolves did. It was their nature. Not something to get riled about.

Not to Tank or Sam.

He took the shovel that the deputy had brought and dug a deep trench and dumped the bodies in it.

"Guess I should say a few words," he said. Then he took a deep breath. "Adios, fuckers," he said.

Then he buried them.

If he'd had the time or the strength, he would've buried Rocky too. The horse deserved a proper burial more than these men did.

"Rocky weren't a believer," Sam said. "But he deserves a good eternity."

He checked out the two horses. Douglas' horse was the better of the two, so he unsaddled her and went to face the unpleasant task of taking the tack off Rocky's body, then taking it and putting it on Douglas' horse. He stashed the saddle and tack in a cleft of rocks.

Then he was ready to return to town. To play dumb and see what happened.

The stable boy, a young Mexican lad, recognized the horses. He saw the questions in the boy's face, but he said nothing. Sam pointed to the one he'd been riding.

"When I leave, this one goes with me. The other I will leave for you. The deputy doesn't need it any longer."

The boy smiled. "And *mi amigo*, Rocky?"

"Muerte," Sam said.

"He will be missed," the boy said.

Sam nodded and left, walking back to the saloon, and walking in the door just after dawn.

Emily was already working in the kitchen. She looked up and let out a breath. "Sit," she said. The coffee she poured for him was hot and dark. He sipped it gratefully and took in her knowing look.

He nodded. "It's done. They are fine, and I sent them home."

"And the—"

"The others won't be coming home. But no one needs to know yet."

She smiled. "You must be hungry. Stove's hot. I'll put on eggs and bacon and beans," she said.

His stomach growled at the prospect. "And a couple of tortillas," he said.

A few minutes later, as he ate, Donna and Amy walked in.

"Looks like everyone wants an early breakfast," Amy said.

"Not that it isn't nice to see you, but are you in town for a reason?" Sam asked.

"A reason? Who the hell needs one of them? I rode back with Elmore because I decided it was a good time to visit my sister," she said. "Sisters do that."

"I'm sure they do. Gives them a chance to catch up on the news."

"And is there any news?" Amy asked.

"There was a jailbreak last night."

"Oh, no!" Donna said. "Them Mexicans got out?"

"Seems so," he said. "Woke me up."

"Anyone hurt?" she asked as Emily brought out steaming plates of food.

"Not that I know of," he said, enjoying the surprise she couldn't hide.

Donna seemed upset. "You go over there?"

"I did. No one was there."

"So, Tank just let them ride out of town?"

"I can't say, Donna," Sam said. "I heard a shot and saw men riding out. I went over in case someone had been shot, but if they were, it wasn't so bad they couldn't ride."

"And you did nothing?" Donna asked. She sounded indignant.

"I'm not the law and I couldn't find the sheriff. I followed them a ways, but they was headed into empty land. It was way too dark to track them and they was riding hard."

"And got clean away?" Amy asked, not seeming to mind as much as Donna.

"Maybe," he said. "Like I said, I came back here."

"Well, I expect the sheriff will catch up with them."

"I don't know how good a tracker he is," Sam said. "Might be. Guess he was good enough to find them in the first place."

"Well, that answers one of your questions," Donna said.

Sam swallowed a forkful of beans and looked at her. "Which question was that, Donna?"

"You wasn't sure our problem was bandits at all. Seems to me, if someone broke them out, then that makes it clear that they were part of a gang of Mexican bandits working in this area."

Sam laughed. "Well, we all know is that there are bandits around. We got Mexican bandits, white outlaw gangs, a couple of black men that robbed a stage in Tucson... The question I had was whether the fellas the sheriff dragged in and beat confessions out of were the ones killing the homesteaders. Just because friends break their amigos out of jail, don't mean the men was guilty. Not of that crime, anyway."

"You are a hard man to satisfy, Sam Colder," Amy said.

Sam smiled. "Not always," he said.

The difference between the sisters was amusing. Donna was having trouble pretending she wasn't angry that Sam hadn't followed the Mexicans. Amy was calm and didn't seem to mind. She had her mind on Sam. But part of that seemed intended to distract him. Maybe she worried that he'd figure out her plan. He couldn't know what was going on inside that head.

"We will have to see how this unfolds," Amy said. "If the sheriff don't catch them bandits and get them back in jail, then there is no telling what might happen. Folks might not be safe."

"That's as true as can be," Sam said.

They ate in silence after that, and when Emily took the plates, Donna stood up. "I got me some work to do, I'm afraid. Elmore has that big order John is gonna need filled."

"Of course," Sam said.

As she left, Amy came to sit next to him. Emily refilled their coffees.

"And what do you have planned for today, Sam Colder?" Amy asked. "More investigating?"

He shook his head. "No. The jailbreak changes things."

"Does it?"

"Yes. I had me an idea, but I got to rethink it. And now I need to be a little extra patient."

"Patient?"

"Got to wait for the sheriff to turn up. When he gets here, maybe we can learn a thing or two about exactly what happened, and what's going on. Don't you want to know if he caught them and what happened?"

"I suppose, but I can't see why that matters," she said. "I mean, what's the difference if he kills them or they just ride off, never to be seen again?"

"You never know what might change things or the way we see things. Sometimes a little fact you knew already becomes more important. Anyway, the jailbreak last night disturbed my sleep and my brain is a little fuzzy. I was thinking about heading over to my room and stretching out for some rest."

She glanced around. "And we need to have a private conversation."

He smiled at her. "Ain't that what we are doing now?"

She leaned forward and put her lips to his ear. "A lot more private than this," she said.

He put a hand on her knee. "Well, I'm not going far. My room is right out back."

She smiled thinly and nodded.

"I was thinking about crawling into my bed until something interesting happens."

Amy smiled and touched his hand. "I bet that if I came by in a few minutes, we could make something interesting happen."

"Could we now?"

Sam drank down the last sip of coffee and stood up. "Well, if you think we need to have a little one-on-one discussion, you know where to find me."

She put her hand to her mouth. "Just don't be in too much rush to go to sleep," she said.

"There are some things that do tend to keep a man awake," he said. "Worrying about money, thinking about some new town. Of course, the promise of a visit from a pretty woman is one of the best."

She smiled, taking it as a compliment.

And maybe it was.

Chapter 20

Amy's Offers

S am got a bottle of whisky and glass from Emily and she squeezed his hand when she handed it to him.

"You did it," she said.

"The good guys get to win sometimes," he said. "We still have some of this left to play out."

Sam took off his gun belt and hung it over the bed. There were still some greedy people around, some who had to be dealt with, but he expected that the gunplay was over for the moment.

The enemies he still had to face favored other weapons. But he had hidden weapons too, and the best one was knowing what had happened out in the desert.

He sat on the bed and took off his boots. Then he poured a drink and let it burn his throat, and wash away the killings. They'd been necessary and there was more hard work to do. It didn't matter whether he wanted to do it or not. This whole mess had to come to a complete stop.

When the door to his room opened, it didn't surprise him to see a woman standing there, posing, waiting for an invitation. It was Amy.

He'd wondered if she'd send Donna, but clearly, it was time for the big guns. The boss was stepping up. It was good to know who ran the show.

She smiled an enticing smile. "Evening, Sam," she said. "Can I come in?"

Returning her smile, he stood up. "I think I'd like that. You care for a drink?"

She came in, turning to close the door, then pausing dramatically, giving him a chance to look her over. Alone like this, with the smell of promise in the air, she was an eyeful, and he didn't mind looking at all. "I don't need a drink. Not right now," she said.

"Waiting for a special occasion?"

"Maybe. I was thinking we might chat a bit."

He went to the window and leaned back against the sill. "Really? You came to my room to chat?"

She moved toward him, and he could smell her perfume. It was flowery, a fake flower smell, though.

"Chatting is a place to start, a way to come to an understanding."

He let that ride.

"I got to thinking that even though you are a smart man, you might not understand every-thing that's going on around here."

"That's entirely possible," he said. "I can be a tad slow at times."

"You know damn well that the ranchers can't afford to let the homesteaders ruin the land with their fences and plows."

"I know they don't like it. What ain't clear is what they are willing to do to stop them, and what that might mean to the governor."

She laughed. "We don't have to do a damn thing. The bandits, Indians, and the life itself will do it for us. It might take time, but they'll all learn how hard life is in this land. And five years? Hell, that's forever out here. They ain't gonna make it. And we see no reason to help them fight a losing battle."

"Life can be hard and short out here," Sam said. "At least for some. Others do all right."

"And you could be one that was doing all right." She licked her lips. "Maybe better than all right."

"Could I now?"

"Sure. But the way you are going, you are at a dead end."

"Am I?"

She moved closer still, inches away now. "With those Mexicans gone, broken out by their pals, it's clear that there is no point in the gov-ernor sending in troops."

"No? They could protect you all."

"Protecting everyone from a small band of Mexicans would spread his troops thin and wouldn't work. And it takes them away from bigger problems. Instead of doing that, he can work with us. We got our hands for protection on the ranches, and if the governor is worried about the homesteaders, he could authorize the sheriff to hire men from Nogales to ride around and protect everyone."

"I'm surprised no one suggested that before now," Sam said. "But you would need the right kind of men. Not outlaws."

"My thought exactly," she said. "John and Elmore are both a little tired of our current sheriff and his attitude. He's an arrogant and nasty man."

"Now there is something we agree on."

"So you could do it."

"Me?"

"We'd make it well worth your while."

"You would?"

"We can send Douglas on his way and give you his job."

"Join you, in other words."

Her tongue danced on her lips. "Sam, fighting each other is such a waste of time."

"So, you'd pay me to be sheriff? I could do that in a bigger town and make more money."

"We could pay more than you think." She reached a hand down and began undoing his pants. "And it wouldn't just be a matter of money. Some personal thanks might be an incentive," she said.

She opened his pants and grabbed his already stiff cock and worked it free.

"See, you are enthusiastic about the benefits of my offer."

"What about your husband?"

"What about him?" she asked.

"He might object to that arrangement."

"What matters to me is that you consider my offer seriously."

Then, with her eyes locked on his, she sank down to her knees, stroking his cock and looking up. Seeing him watching her, his eyes on her lips, she smiled and licked the head of his cock.

"A little taste, for me," she laughed. "A sample, for you."

Then she opened her mouth and took his swollen cock in it.

He leaned back, watching her face as she sucked his cock, using her tongue and lips in combination to arouse him, to tease him. He touched her head, enjoying seeing her going down on him.

She worked him good, arousing him until he couldn't hold back any longer. Then he held her head tight against him and came, shooting his cum down her throat. She choked on the flood of semen and he released her.

As his cock softened, she smiled up at him. "Like I said, a taste, a sample."

"Are we negotiating?" he asked. "That was nice, but…"

"But what?" she asked.

"I think you want more from me than keeping order in Rock Canyon."

"Like what?" she asked.

Sam pushed his pants down and stepped out of them.

"You aren't going to be happy being the wife of the big deal rancher, Amy."

"Why do you say that?"

"You didn't give me a blow job and promise more because you want your husband to win this little war. That's not near enough."

"What do you think I want?"

"To be the boss."

Her smile mixed surprise with cunning. "Is that what I want? And how would I get it?"

"By making sure I was your sheriff, not his. By having me use these men I hire to protect everyone."

"To do what?"

"They might see that John Chancellor and maybe Mayor Redding both have unfortunate accidents that leave their widows in charge."

He gave her credit for not immediately pretending shock.

"Well, that's an interesting idea, Sam Colder. You've clearly given it some thought. And I can see why."

"Why?"

"Because with them gone, you'd be the rooster in the henhouse. That would leave you set up nice, too."

Sam began undoing the buttons on her dress.

"What are you doing, Sam?" she asked, staring at him as he yanked it down her shoulders, exposing her breasts. Despite the protesting nature of her words, she pulled her shoulders back to give him an eyeful.

"I'm getting on with exactly what you came here for. I'm getting you naked so I can fuck you."

She lifted her chin in a haughty look. "Then we have a deal?"

"I been auditioning for my part since I got here, Amy. I been showing you and your sister that I can handle tough men and I showed her I can handle a horny woman. I'm sure she's told you that. Now it's time for you to show me that you can please me."

"You think I can't?"

He heard uncertainty in her voice for the first time.

Yanking the dress down her hips, he took her by the arms and pushed her back onto his bed, and ran his hands over her body, spreading her legs apart and staring at her cunt.

"I aim to find out what you can do, what you will do to get my help," he said. "If we are gonna be partners, well, our arrangement better satisfy us both."

He wasn't that interested in giving her pleasure at all, but Sam wanted her and he did the thing that would get his prick hard again fast—he put his face down to her steaming slit. His hands grabbed her legs, lifting them, and he ran his tongue through the pink furrow.

She gasped and her hands touched his head, pressing his face tight against her.

"Oh, Sam!" she moaned as he worked his fingers into her, fucking her with them as he used his tongue to explore her fleshy folds.

Her moans of pleasure told him he was finding the spots he had been hunting. Then he worked her body, following the sign, exciting her. Feeling the tremors of passion rippling through her body, listening to her gasps, the sudden inhales of breath told him he'd struck gold.

By the time he felt her explode, bucking under him like some saddle bronc, he was ready. He pushed her legs back to her ears and drove his rigid pole into that wet, hot channel, burying it in her. His face found a breast, and he sucked a nipple, getting it rock hard as he slammed into her, fucking her hard. She was still buzzing from coming when he ate her, and soon enough, the deep penetration of his thrusts had her coming again.

Not so explosive this time, but still losing control.

He pounded into her until her vibrations slowed, then he pulled out and rolled her onto her knees.

"What?"

Sam slapped her ass with a stinging blow. She cried out, and he got behind her, admiring the red mark on her ass cheek as he guided his stiff cock to her tight little anus and centered it there.

"No, Sam!" she cried, but he was already leaning into her, pushing the head through the tight sphincter and into her ass. He took her roughly, stretching her ass with his swollen cock.

She had her ass in the air and her face in the sheets, whimpering slightly, but also moaning now.

"Your sister must get ass fucked more than you do," he told her. "Her ass isn't nearly so tight. Maybe the sheriff uses it hard."

"Bastard!" she cried.

Then he came, emptying his balls, and shooting his cum up her rectum.

When he slipped out of her, she rolled over, looking at him, trying to decide if she'd won or lost that round.

"So, we have a deal?" she asked.

"There are still some things to sort out," he said.

She scowled. "Like what? Either you'll be our sheriff or not."

"Well, if we do what you proposed, Sheriff Douglas won't go quietly."

"Then you can deal with him."

"And Tank?"

She smiled and stretched out on the bed, being seductive. The woman wanted more.

"I don't think he'll be a problem."

"That still leaves me with a couple of things to think about before I give my word."

"Tell me," she said. "I can help."

"These are things I need to figure out myself. A good night's sleep and I'll know. We can go over it all in the morning," he said.

"John is coming to town tonight," she said. "He will be here in an hour or so. I can't stay the night."

Sam pretended to be disappointed.

"Then it's a good thing I insisted on the bigger sample this morning."

"You sonofabitch," she said, but she was smiling and she reached over to stroke his cock.

She'd liked the rough fuck, being forced to take it in the ass. She probably wanted it rougher than that, but more important to her, she was sure she had him hooked.

"Make sure everyone comes to the saloon for breakfast tomorrow morning," he said.

"Everyone? Donna and I—"

"Everyone."

"Why?"

"Because I hate starting the day without a good meal."

That set her back. "Why have everyone there?"

"There are some things we need to establish. I got to work out what I'll tell the governor and I want everyone to know where they stand, what they might need to do."

She scowled. "Even John?"

"And the mayor."

"And the sheriff?"

"If he's back in town by then, sure. But he might be busy elsewhere."

That puzzled her.

"Why don't you think he'll be back?"

Sam ran a hand over her bare thigh. "Because I suspect he'll have trouble making it back soon."

"You are being vague."

"It is deliberate."

"What about my proposal?"

He stroked her ass. "Once I hold my little town meeting, if the offer is still on the table, we can come in here and discuss it privately."

"I don't understand, but okay."

"Now go back to your sister's place unless you want John to find out what's going on before you are ready for him to know."

"If we do it right, he'll never find out," she said.

There was malice in her eyes, but she directed it at the thought of John Chancellor, her husband.

"If I do what you want, he won't ever find out anything else again," Sam said.

She got up from the bed, smelling of sex, and began dressing.

"We can do a lot more of this once he's gone," she said.

"I'm working on the assumption that regular fucking is part of the deal you are offering," Sam said. "So, if I'm wrong, best let me know now."

She bent down and kissed him. "You ain't wrong at all. And if you are willing to use that tongue on me like that, you can have whatever you want."

As she left, Sam thought about how clear things were now. Amy had been behind it all—the murders, the framing of the Mexicans, the attempt at grabbing all the land. She and her sister were running that show. Chancellor was a stooge. The mayor knew more, but they had him under their thumb.

It was bothersome that he hadn't seen it. Maybe he didn't find it easy to think of a woman as someone who would do all that.

And he had to admit that it annoyed him to find that one person could be so sexy, so smart, and so evil all at the same time. He'd enjoyed fucking her.

But now that he had, he didn't want to do it again.

It didn't seem right somehow.

Chapter 21

Breakfast

Sam didn't rush getting up the next morning, but he'd rested the day before. After Amy left, he fell asleep for a few hours and then treated himself to a lazy day.

It had been interesting to note that no one seemed to be worried about the sheriff and his deputy. There wasn't a suggestion of sending anyone out looking for them. They wouldn't be missed, sorely or otherwise.

And this morning, when he dressed and came into the saloon for breakfast, they were all there. The whole fucking clan of weasels.

Emily was cooking eggs and sausage and serving people. The smell of coffee suggested that the day had half a chance of getting off to a good start.

Emily gave him an inquiring look as she handed him his coffee.

"Stay close," he said. "Should be some interesting conversations this morning."

"I still ain't seen the sheriff this morning," Donna said.

"He must still be chasing down those prisoners," John Chancellor said. "Colder, can you shed any light on what's going on around here?"

"I can. And for now, well, the sheriff ain't that important to the matters at hand," Sam said. "He ain't no more than a hired gun, and as it happens, I can tell you why he ain't here."

"You know where he is?" John Chancellor asked.

"I'll get to all that," Sam said.

He motioned to them all. So, I'll tell you what I'm gonna be telling the governor in a few days. It's quite a story."

As Sam laid out his tale of how the sheriff, Chancellor's man, had hired men to kill the homesteaders and ambush Sam, he grew certain that Chancellor was totally in the dark.

"Why would he do that?"

"Because he was an outlaw, and one your wife hired to do those things, John. She couldn't count on you to chase off the homesteaders, so she took care of it."

"That's absurd!" Amy said. A confused look distorted her face.

"It's okay, Amy," Sam said. "Like you said, we got to settle the whole thing, resolve it for everyone. So let me do it." He turned back to Chancellor. "She saw that the world was changing. The government gave them land you needed, and they weren't going to leave easy. Now I'm sure you guessed some of it, but it weren't in your interest to say a damn thing."

"That's fucking crazy," Mayor Redding said. "The sheriff said the Mexicans…"

"They were just convenient." Sam reached out and patted Amy's hand. "I'm guessing that was Amy's idea, too. She is the brains behind this. Although Douglas might have come up with it. It's his kind of bluff."

"Why would I want that?" she asked, looking pale.

"When the governor got wind of the killings, he wanted to take action. You had the sheriff grab some Mexicans to blame it on to keep him from sending troops."

"Sheriff Douglas said he had evidence," Amy said.

"And my investigation was fucking that up. I've got witnesses to some of the events, and I think he guessed that. That's when Amy, or Donna more likely, convinced the sheriff that the bandits had to escape. Did you have to fuck him to convince him to take them out into the desert to kill them, or was he happy to do it for his wages?"

"What?" Donna sat up straight.

"However you sold the idea, he set it up so I'd follow them out to a spot they'd picked where Tank could ambush me. I guess they thought a second attempt would go better."

"The deputy?" Chancellor asked.

"That's right. But I killed him and sent the prisoners, innocent men, home. Meantime, Douglas rode off intending to kill everyone at the Holloway homestead."

Chancellor was puffing now. "Why the hell would he do that?"

"Well, officially he wouldn't. That's why the Mexicans had to appear to escape. He intended to come back and say the bandits did it on their way out of here." He looked at Amy. "Did I get that right? Anyway, Douglas shot Holloway, but he didn't kill him. When I got there, Douglas was about to set fire to their cabin, to burn them out. He didn't want to be reasonable, so I killed him, too."

"You killed both of them?" the mayor asked.

"And buried them both out in the desert."

The table was quiet then.

"That's what you'll tell the governor?" Amy asked.

"Yup."

Amy smiled. "Colder, you don't have a shred of proof that any of that happened. None of us is going to testify against the others and it will be the word of this community against yours."

Sam rubbed his chin. "Let's see, the Holloways will testify about the attack on their place and the confession Douglas made while he was doing it. The family of the so–called bandits will support my story, and, by the way, one of them saw Douglas and his men attack the Walker place. So, maybe I can make a case."

"That's bullshit," Amy said. "You are making things up."

"Well, it isn't likely I can get any charges filed against any of you that will make a difference. But that's all right. The governor knew this was a land dispute and nothing the courts could settle. He'd prefer it got settled out of court because range wars are popping up like wildfires and they just have to be stamped out."

"What does that mean?" Chancellor asked. "What gets settled?"

"Most likely, the governor will take my suggestion that he ask John Chancellor to take responsibility for the safety of the homesteaders. As a favor. He will send down an honest sheriff who will enforce the law and protect everyone, ranchers and homesteaders alike."

"That's it?" Chancellor asked. He smelled an escape, and Sam sensed he was ready to grab it.

"It will have to do," Sam said. "The men that were doing the dirty work are all dead, except maybe one who left these parts with my bullet in him and won't likely be back. Your wife wasted your money on a bad bunch of thugs, John."

"What the fuck were you doing, Amy?" Chancellor asked.

She waved a hand. "John, you been screaming about how the ranch wasn't going to grow without that grazing land," she said. "You weren't doing anything to save what we built. You didn't have the balls to do what needed to be done, so I stepped up."

"What I built," Chancellor said. Then he sat back, his eyes half closed. "I guess I have been closing my eyes to what's going on around here."

"You make that sound like you wasn't paying attention, John," Sam said. "You're as full of bullshit as your wife. When we talked at your place, I laid it out for you, and you sounded pretty damn happy it was happening. When you keep a pet snake, don't pretend to be shocked when it bites you on the ass."

His scowl deepened. "Well, is there anything else I should know?" He glared at his wife. "Anything else you can tell me?"

Sam sipped his coffee, finishing the last cold sip. Then he put the cup down.

"I'm going to leave in a few minutes," Sam said. "I'm going to leave you folks to sort out what you do... to each other as well as in terms of discussion with the governor, but before I leave, I want to warn you, John, and you, Mayor Redding, that you might want to watch your backs. The plans the ladies were talking to me about involved you two having shorter and more tragic futures than either of you would hope for yourself. She hired one man to take care of that and was looking to replace him with me."

Redding jumped out of his chair. "Donna?"

His wife shot him a sharp look. "Don't be an ass, Elmore," she said. "You are making a fool of yourself."

"You already made a fool of him, Donna," Sam said. "You got him playing your stupid game and even though he kept his mouth shut, you still cuckolded him with the sheriff and me."

The mayor turned white. "Donna!"

Chancellor laughed. "I always knew you were a weakling, Redding. Unable to keep your wife in line."

Sam stood up and slapped Chancellor on the shoulders. "But, before you laugh too hard at Mayor Redding, John, I want you to know that your Amy is also a fine and willing fuck. And, for future reference, last night, she learned that she loves taking a hard cock in her ass."

Then he walked out, unsure if someone would call out, or even pull a gun. But they were all tied up in their own knots, wondering exactly what would happen next to them. He'd only sketched things out for them. Now they'd sort out whether they fought it out or tried to work together to save themselves.

And Sam realized that he didn't give a shit. He'd done his job, done as much as he could to bring a little justice to Rock Canyon. It wasn't perfect, but what the hell was? A hot night in Tucson, maybe.

Now it was time to move on.

Chapter 22

Departure

S am left the saloon and stopped on the boardwalk to roll a cigarette. Outside that room, with angry, accusing voices beginning to rise with the heat of morning, the air was a lot fresher. Cleaner.

"Well, you sure stirred that pot up real nice," Emily said, coming outside and standing beside him.

He smiled at her grin. "You think I did?"

"The only bad part is that the law won't come down on them."

"Why not?"

She laughed. "Because from the sound of things, those folks are gonna tear each other's throats out before the law has a chance to do shit to any of them."

Sam laughed and lit his cigarette, drawing in a long hit of the smoke. "Well, that's fine with me."

"Me, too," she said. "Whatever happens around here next, I figure it's the end of Rock Canyon, though. Least for me. If the Chancellors aren't prospering, there ain't much to keep the town going. Not that I'd want to stay, anyway. I'm done with these good people."

"What will you do?" he asked.

She smiled. "Does it matter?"

"It does to me."

She studied his face for a moment, then nodded. "I been thinking I'd head over Nogales way. I got a sister there I ain't seen in some time. She and her husband got themselves a store. Maybe they could use some help."

Sam nodded. "Need any help getting there? I was going to Tucson, but I could make a side trip if you want."

She looked up at him. "You'd do that for me, wouldn't you?"

"If I could. If you asked."

Her hand touched his arm. "You're a good man. But no thanks. I kinda want to watch some of this play out before I head off. I can find my way. Besides, I could get sweet on you."

"Would that be a bad thing?"

She laughed. "For both of us, Sam."

They stood together for a time, then Sam walked slowly down toward the stable.

The stable boy had seen him coming and as Sam approached, he walked Mark Douglas' horse out. She wore Rocky's saddle and looked freshly groomed.

When he took the reins from the boy, handing him a coin, he stared into the horse's face and his chest tightened. This wasn't his horse. Rocky was his horse, not this nag.

The boy tugged at his sleeve.

"Mister, I know she ain't the horse you rode here, and he was special, but this here is a splendid animal. She has a grand and noble nature. Please don't blame her for the evil things his owner did. What happened to Rocky ain't her fault."

Sam cursed himself silently, then turned to look into the eager young face.

"Ain't you the smart one? That's exactly what I was working myself up to do all right, and it's damn stupid and wrong. I thank you for that reminder. This horse didn't pick her owner, but fate brought us together, so I guess we both got to make the most of it."

The boy nodded and pocketed the coin. Then he took off his hat and gave Sam a solemn look.

"The men you saved were my uncles," he said. He glanced around. "Are they are safe now?"

"Yes. Your whole family is safe. The ranchers don't know who they are and have no reason to come after them. That was the sheriff, and he is dead."

"Then my family sends you their thanks and their wishes for the blessings of God."

Then, before he could even digest what the boy said, he disappeared.

Sam turned to the horse. He held her by the hackamore and stroked her nose, staring into the big, soft eyes. There was spirit in them. It danced in her eyes.

"I don't know what name he gave you," he said. "But I killed the sonofabitch. So now, we are going to be partnering up, and I want to give you one of my own. I like that spirit. So I'd like to call you Dancer. If that's okay."

When she whinnied, Sam took it for approval.

"Good, then." He put a foot in the stirrup and swung up into the saddle, hearing the creak of the leather. It was a different seat than being on Rocky.

He clucked and Dancer started off down the street. "We're headed northwest," he told her. "To Tucson. It's a ways, but we'll have us some fun there, then head up to Prescott and see if Claire answered my letter."

Dancer snorted and took several high steps in the direction of the distant horizon.

Donna had one thing right in her vision of things. The world was changing. Even Sam was changing. He'd spent the last days helping to assert civilization's hold on this little town, and yet, he wasn't part of that civilized world. He wasn't a proper part of either the lawlessness that once ruled or the civilization riding the rails west.

It was certain this wouldn't be the last time he'd have to take a side in that battle, and he didn't see good always sitting on one side or the other.

But now, thoughts of Tucson called to him. He and Dancer would ride that distance and get to know each other out here. Away from the railroads and towns, life and death came and went quickly and without much fuss. Rocky and the sheriff and his men were all permanent guests of the high desert now. One day, he'd probably join them. But none of those deaths would change much.

The desert, at least for now, was still bigger and stronger than any man, and Sam Colder managed to take a fair amount of comfort from that.

While it stayed true.

THE END

Next in the series
Gold Town Bandits

Coming down out of the Black Hills, heading out of Arizona and down toward Mule Creek, New Mexico, the country opened into wide vistas of open scrub land.

The dry season was just starting, and the brittlebrush was still in bloom, turning the hillsides orange and yellow.

Atop a small hill, Sam Colder dismounted and took a small poke from his saddlebags. His weathered fingers picked some brittlebrush, stuffing the bag full. The stems made fine toothbrushes, and the gum from the resin also could be heated and applied to the chest to cure chest pains.

The plant didn't grow above about 4,000 feet and he intended to spend some time in the mountains well above that altitude, so he would stock up now, while he had a chance.

It was all part of living in the moment. And the moment was a rather pretty one and the view from the hill was lovely.

Dancer snorted. "Bet you smell water," he said. It had been a thirsty ride, and she deserved a drink. Mounting up, Sam pointed her to Mule Spring, not far away, just this side of Mule Creek.

As the name implied, Mule Spring was where travelers stopped to water their mules. Water could be sketchy most places in the southwest, but often enough, Mule Spring rewarded its visitors by providing some—at least enough to quench parched lips. It was a gamble, but a lot better one than other options. And if Dancer said there was water, he was sure he'd find some.

Best of all, heading that way didn't even take him out of his way. The outlaw he had been tracking ever since he picked up his sign just outside of Safford would need water worse than Sam and Dancer. The man had lit out, on the run, without preparation, whereas Sam and Dancer had both slept the night before under shelter and had left with full canteens.

A thirsty man on the run, one who knew much of anything, was sure to head that way. If not, it would be easy enough to find his sign again after they took a break.

The spring sat in a small depression. When they arrived, Sam Colder found that Dame Fortune was smiling on them. Even from a distance, he could see the outlaw's horse standing in the shallow water, drinking. Slipping down off Dancer and telling her to wait just a bit longer, Sam drew his Colt, and rotated the cylinder, putting the hammer over a chamber with a round in it. Then he slowly moved closer.

His caution was wasted. He walked up to find Stan Baker, the travel-weary outlaw he was chasing, lying face down in the shallow muddy water, inhaling it. Seemingly intent on drinking every last drop, Baker didn't notice Sam's approach, or even hearing the cocking of Sam's pistol. He was making this arrest a rather pleasant affair.

Sam waited politely for the man to finish and even to let out a sigh of relief.

"Okay, Stan, now that you've guzzled down most of the water left in the territory, roll over on your back, keeping your hands well away from your guns," Sam said.

The man twitched and then looked back over his shoulder.

"Fuck," he said, his eyes rolling back after one glance at the business end of Sam's Colt. Then he stretched his arms out over his head and rolled over, showing Sam a mud-encrusted beard.

"Don't move till I say," Sam told him.

"No worry about me, mister. There ain't no bullets in my gun," the man said.

"No?"

"Hard to believe, but that fucking deputy only had four in the gun and there weren't none in his saddlebags."

"Careless of him. And you fired three of those shells when you made your escape."

"Did I now?"

Sam nodded. "I was told you put two in the deputy and then fired a third as you mounted up."

"I wanted people to keep their heads down."

"Didn't work. You hit a woman in the general store."

"Shit! She okay?"

"Not unless being dead is okay. Your bullet took most of the back of her head off."

"I didn't know she was there."

"Even if I believe you, that tells me you still have one bullet left. One in the right place is plenty."

The man turned his head away. "Last night, I shot at a rabbit."

"Well, the thing is, after what you did to that deputy in Safford, I don't think I want to take your word for that. I hope you understand."

"He was taking me to face that fucking judge for stealing a horse. I told the deputy I didn't do it, but he didn't want to listen to me any more than anyone else did. He said to save it for the judge."

"And instead of doing that, making your case to a judge, you decided to murder two people. Funny how some folks can manage to make bad shit smell worse."

"You must know me, Mister," he said, his laugh weak.

Sam approached to finish this off. The man didn't move a muscle as he bent down and pulled the revolver from the man's belt. It was an old gun and not well maintained. When he opened it, he found four empty cartridges and one empty cylinder. He hadn't lied about that.

"Are you telling me that the deputy was escorting you to trial carrying this piece of shit gun and with only four bullets?"

Stan smiled, proud of his achievement. "I yanked that sucker right out of his belt and put a round in his belly before he could even think what to do."

Sam tossed the gun aside. "I'm surprised it didn't blow your hand off when you fired it."

He shook his head. "Once I had a chance to take a look at the damn thing, I had that very thought. But I never woulda guessed a lawman would pack such garbage. And given what was happening, even if I'd known, I don't think it would have changed things."

"I do understand desperation, Mr. Baker. Of course, now you are gonna go back to face the original charge, and then, unless they hang you right away, you'll stand another trial for murdering the deputy and that lady."

That didn't seem to upset him. "So, you are planning to take me straight back to Safford?"

"That's where the judge is waiting for you. And he's getting mighty impatient, I hear tell."

"Now?"

"Now. And seeing as we got us about sixty miles to ride together, I'm going to give you one choice."

"A choice?" Baker cocked his head. He smelled a ray of hope.

"You can choose to make the trip the easy way or the hard way."

"What's the hard way?"

"Tied over your saddle like I was bringing in a dead man."

"Ugh."

"If you behave yourself, I'll tie your hands and you can sit in the saddle like a living man."

"Fine. Cause, I'm done running," he said. He looked forlorn. "It came to me while I was riding here."

"Came to you?"

"Yeah. I saw I was making a mad dash to nowhere. I was riding like hell and trying to decide whether to head north or south. Then I knew it didn't fucking matter one damn bit. This child has got nowhere to go and nothing to do when he gets there. I made my escape, but all

I got away with was a tired horse, a shit pistol, and saddlebags full of nothing."

He wasn't lying. His face sagged, showing how the fight had gone out of him. The hopelessness of his situation was getting to him. That sense of defeat might not last, but it was something you could work with for a time.

Sam tied Stan's wrists together with some rawhide strands and sat him by a tree.

"What now?" the man asked.

"I want to water my horse, if you left her any."

"I've never been so damn thirsty. The fucking deputy didn't even have a canteen for either of us."

"Foolish of him."

But then the deputy had been foolish enough to let his prisoner get his gun. He'd been foolish enough to carry that piece of shit pistol in the first place, and trying to escort a prisoner when he only had four bullets.

As far as the deputy went, all bets were off. He'd have to have a talk with the sheriff in Safford when he got back, maybe put a burr under his saddle and get him to take a better look at his deputies. This man gave law enforcement a bad name.

With the horses watered, Sam helped Stan on his horse, got up on Dancer, and headed toward Safford.

"You got any food with you?" Stan asked.

"Some. But you said you ate a rabbit."

"No. I said I fired the gun at a rabbit." He twisted up his face. "I was so fucking hungry, I missed him completely."

"You don't know how to set a snare?"

"Not so you'd notice. Besides, I knew the posse would be after me."

"How can a man living out here not know how to make a snare?"

Baker shrugged. "I ain't one of you god-damn mountain men., you know. I spent my life working cows."

"And you've never lived off the land?"

"Shit no. The boss provides me with food and gives me a bunk and a dollar a month and I work his cattle, mend fences, and do shit like that."

It made a little sense. A man generally learned what he needed to know, but this kind of lapse bothered Sam. This was the frontier and people fended for themselves. The ones who survived did.

"Well, if we get moving, we can probably make it to Owl Creek with enough daylight left to set us some snares and have a decent meal," Sam told him.

"What's wrong with right here?" Baker asked.

"Time," Sam said. "There ain't no sense in wasting daylight sitting here."

He twisted in the saddle so he could dig into his saddlebag and fished out some jerky and tearing off a decent piece that he handed to Baker. Even with his hands tied together, he could eat it, and he tore into it.

"When we get to the Gila River, follow it, we should find plenty of game."

Stan wolfed down the jerky and then settled into a peaceful silence. The horses seemed to like getting back up into the mountains again, and they made decent time without pushing. After about five hours, they came in sight of the cottonwoods that grew along the Gila River.

They reined in the horses, and Sam looked around. They seemed to be alone.

"Owl Creek is a few miles to the west," Sam said. "We will camp there and I'll fix you a decent meal."

"How about I help you hunt something?" Stan asked.

Sam laughed. "Much as I appreciate the help, I think I'll let you sit by the fire, hogtied."

The man shrugged. "You got to try."

"I'm doing you a favor," Sam said.

"How's that?"

"You said you were tired of running, so I'm making sure you can't do any more of it."

"What a pal," Stan said. He snorted. "I never thought of a lawman as being such a helpful cuss."

"I'm not a lawman," Sam said. Then he gave Stan a stern look. "I'm a bounty hunter and you best keep that in mind."

"What's the difference to me?" Stan asked.

Sam shrugged. "Well, it means I get paid the same for bringing you in dead as alive."

"Sheriff wins that way too."

"But, since I don't need to think about getting re-elected, I don't have to worry about disappointing folks by bringing a man in dead and cheating them of a hanging."

Stan's smile faded. "I didn't think of that. Fucking politics."

"I can't disagree," Sam said.

READ THE REST AT
https://books2read.com/u/mgNXoX

About Kurt Dysan

<u>Kurt Dysan</u> lives in the great southwestern US and loves exploring the rural areas that were once New Mexico and Arizona Territories. Stories of the old West are still alive there.

You can reach Kurt at
Kurt_dysan@yahoo.ca
You can find his other books and stories at:

https://books2read.com/ap/nBYawR/Kurt-Dysan